Heaven Scent Hunter

The Agarwood Adventure

by

Ron Austin

Table of Contents

Characters

Dr. Alan Grace: PhD biology, son of David Grace.

David Grace: Business manager for Batari Royal Family.

Betty: MSc. Alan's grad student, research assistant, and general mage.

Harry Dunlap: Head of US clandestine operations in Southeast Asia.

Sakda: Maran village elder, jungle and agarwood expert. Grand-uncle of Leng.

Leng: Alan's plantation manager. Son of Tevy. Sakda's surrogate son.

Kareem: King of Batar. Father of Nazneen. Alan's patron.

Nazneen: Batari princess and businesswoman. Daughter of Kareem.

Yuying Li: Chinese agarwood expert. Nicknamed Wylie. Daughter of Heng.

Fan: Yuying's bodyguard.

Keat Chhon: Senior Cambodian police officer.

Humboldt: American embassy employee and spy.

Rithy: The chief of the Khmer Loeu, a hill tribe remnant group.

Tevy: Plantation cook. Leng's mother. Sakda's niece.

Kapono: Plantation worker. Maran villager.

Sgt. Samphy and **Kosal**: Cambodian police officers.

Quentin T. Wilkes: CEO, SpringenRx.

Paula Bondwell: Commissioner, FDA (Food and Drug Administration)

Dr. Armand: French physician, Doctors without Borders/Médecins Sans Frontières (MSF)

Ken: Documentary filmmaker. Narrator of the prologue and epilogue.

Prologue

I was in the hot, humid Eastern Bus Terminal in Bangkok waiting for a midafternoon bus to Trat in southeastern Thailand. The minibus rolled in; I gave the driver my pack and grabbed a seat. A handsome, intelligent-looking young guy wearing cargo pants, sandals, and an Angkor Beer T-shirt sat beside me.

"Where ya from?" I asked. The minibus pulled away, and the air conditioning kicked in.

The man closed his eyes, and his nostrils flared. Then he opened his eyes with a little headshake, looked right at me, and smiled. "America. You?"

"Canada. I'm Ken … on my way to Koh Chang." (Elephant Island.)

"I love Koh Chang."

"Me too. Great place to recover from dental surgery." I rubbed my sore jaw. "Your name?"

"Alan. Going to Cambodia."

"Cambodia? Cool! Vacation?"

Alan laughed. "No, I am finishing my thesis. On agarwood."

"Garwood?"

"A, G, A, R, agarwood. It is a special and precious dark wood. Worth more than gold."

"Never heard of the agarwood tree."

"It comes from a few kinds of trees here in Asia, but it's not a species. Some trees get infected or injured, and the tree makes oil to heal. It's used for incense, perfume, and sometimes carving."

"Wow. Tell me more."

And he did. For almost six hours on the way to Trat.

In turn, and in between parts of his yarn, I told him my story. "I make documentary films, and I've won some awards. I made *Infopreneur*." An unexpected hit about the dot-com boom on the then-exploding internet, it was one of those few documentaries to break through and make some money.

"*Infopreneur*. I remember it. Very cool."

I asked more questions. Alan's PhD focused on improving the quality of domesticated agarwood; he hoped to end the massive clear-cuts in Southeast Asian forests. He was headed for his father's plantation in Cambodia where they were finding new ways to cultivate agarwood.

"Your father's plantation?"

"Long story." He smiled. "My father managed the business affairs for King Kareem and the royal family of Batar." (One of the small Arabian Gulf kingdoms.) "I often traveled with him as a young boy, played in the palace with his daughter, Princess Nazneen. The king introduced me to agarwood, even gave me a carving." Alan held up the amulet around his neck. "My dad purchased and set up a plantation for the king. Then bought land for himself and retired to grow agarwood."

So far, the tale was a documentary-worthy story in itself. Then Alan told me about the jungle hunt for wild agarwood and the ruthless kill-or-be-killed smuggling that sent the contraband to the wealthy collectors in China, Japan, and the Arab world. I was ready to write a feature-film screenplay.

We finally got to Trat, ending my life-changing bus ride. The bus terminal was cooler than the one in Bangkok and full of conflicting aromas, which seemed to distract Alan.

"I'd like to make a documentary," I said, "about agarwood, with you."

He refocused on me. "Great idea."

We made a few plans, exchanged contact information, and parted ways.

***

 After two weeks on Koh Chang—a tropical paradise not quite overrun by tourists back then and great for beach walks, swims, and Thai food—I was recharged. To prepare for the new documentary, I'd researched agarwood on the web. I needed to augment my travel pack of camcorders, so I arranged to rent some serious video equipment from Bangkok, picked it up in Trat, and headed for the Hat-Lek/Koh Kong border crossing into Cambodia.

Welcome to Cambodia

Six Years Later

Alan Grace closed the door of his old Land Cruiser with an extra shove, fondled a dark wooden amulet attached to his key ring, and sniffed. He processed the various smells of the border crossing, tried to ignore the sting of rotting durian fruit, and headed toward the gate near the modest Cambodian immigration and customs building. The border post was about ten kilometers north of the town of Koh Kong on the east coast of the Gulf of Thailand.

He weaved his way through the jumble of touts, street vendors, and feisty taxi and tuk-tuk drivers already hard at work in the early morning and put some money in the bowl of an old legless beggar. Then he stopped and inhaled the incense smoke from a little shrine wafting his favorite scent. He struggled to maintain focus, ever the victim of his rare condition, hyperosmia, an increased olfactory acuity. Alan had a super nose, an organ so sensitive it could be a problem.

He closed his eyes and counted. He reopened them, saw a Day-Glo purple truck with paragliding gear in the back. An attractive blond couple were having a nasty argument as they drove through the customs gate. Seeing the elaborate gear triggered thrilling memories tinged with melancholy; he'd given up paragliding years ago to get serious about his academic pursuits in biology. The couple stopped, got out, and continued to exchange insults in an incomprehensible Scandinavian-sounding language. Then he realized it *was* English they were yelling at each other, but a heavily accented variety. They were from different countries and needed English to communicate … and fight. How could they be so unhappy? They were arriving in Cambodia to go gliding. He shook his head, looked back. Thai gamblers came through the gate mixed with *barang* backpackers, temple tourists, and porters.

Betty, his slightly nerdy ex-grad student, emerged from the border zone and waved at Alan. Her good mood infected just about

4

everyone she passed by. She, alongside two porters with large handcarts, pulled an enormous set of luggage. Alan gulped then smiled and gave her a big hug; by holding his breath, he managed to delay and reduce the effect of her scent.

"I've got your Greenie."

Alan smiled. *Celestial Fragrances* had won the award for Best Eco-Documentary.

"I accepted it for you, with Ken. He says hi."

"Thanks." He was pleased with the win and his proactive protégé. They had a great partnership. He was grateful and delighted to have his best friend and indispensable assistant join him in this remote corner of the world.

"Still sorry about your dad."

He nodded. She'd already consoled him months ago when David Grace had died of a sudden heart attack, but they hadn't seen each other in the meantime. Alan took one of her bags and led them to his vehicle. It was soon full, so the porters piled the rest on top and expertly tied it down.

Alan paid them. Were they sons of the men who'd transported weapons for the Khmer Rouge to fight the Vietnamese army? They'd used this same route back in the eighties, before the agarwood plantations were established in the nineties by Alan's father. But these men were too young; more likely they were the grandsons. There weren't many old people in Cambodia. The rooftop load swayed a bit as they pulled away and left the border area.

Betty and Alan approached the town of Koh Kong, slowed for tuk-tuks, pedestrians, cyclists, and school children while the motorbikes weaved through the traffic and passed them.

Betty said, "Wow, Cambodia. Hey, Professor, I've graduated to field work."

Alan nodded. They drove in silence for a few minutes, getting used to each other again.

Betty broke the silence. "Hey, I looked up *farang*. You know what it means?"

"White person, or foreigner."

"White devil." Betty grinned ear to ear. "I'm a farang, a white devil."

"I've heard that too." Alan chuckled. "But that's Thai. There's no *f* sound in Khmer. Here in Cambodia you're a barang. Originally it meant French, according to some."

Betty was impressed by the scenery and the exotic sights but shocked at the amount of garbage in many places. Alan, long since inured to the scene outside their windows, had other concerns. When his father died, he'd been on the cusp of a major breakthrough in his university lab: perfecting a distilling process whereby plantation-grown agarwood would render a product almost equal to the oil derived from wild agarwood. A death in the family meant all other concerns were put aside. Alan flew immediately to Phnom Penh and spent a couple of weeks dealing with the funeral, the will, and reorganizing the plantation. He appointed his bright young Cambodian friend Leng to manage things, formalizing Leng's leadership role, then got ready to go home.

Completely baffled when the university launched its fraud accusations, he blamed academic jealousy and his poor political skills. He decided to stay in Cambodia to pursue his urgent scientific quest, built a jungle lab, and continued his research at the plantation. He basically ignored the fraud charges and seemed to have abandoned his university lab and students.

His good mood faded. "You have the data?"

"The data is safe," Betty said.

"What do you mean?"

"It's gone way beyond SpringenRx and 'academic fraud.'"

"It worked, got rid of me."

"So why did men-in-black guards lock out milquetoast grad students?

Alan stared. "You got locked out of the biology lab?"

"Yup. And they embargoed all the project's servers and data banks behind Cisco firewalls. The data itself was zirconium encrypted!"

"Data about trees—"

"Took me more than twenty minutes to break in and crack it!" She paused. "This is it, isn't it? … CIA?" He didn't react. Her voice went up a register. "NSA?"

"SpringenRx's funding conditions?" A more mundane motive.

Betty, eyes wide, in her highest pitched voice, said, "Blackwater shadow ops!"

"Why would they care about agarwood trees?"

"We are so ready for this!"

Alan had often dismissed Betty's beliefs. Now he laughed. "Your paranoia finally pays off: embargoed biology." But then he shuddered. What was going on?

He had to stop; the traffic was blocked by a group of saffron-robed monks. Flanked by happy people giving alms, the monks burned incense and chanted on the road ahead.

Alan started a U-turn, looking for a quick escape. Behind them the road was blocked, and people had deserted their vehicles and joined the crowd. "Should've taken the other road." The incense smoke had distracted him.

"What *is* this?" Betty said.

"Looks like a blessing ceremony for a new business. Must be a big business…"

Betty escaped the Land Cruiser and joined the monks and spectators—a tall, smiling, fair-haired westerner among the shorter, smiling Cambodians.

Chagrin turned to amusement. *Field work!*

A loud siren shocked everyone, and an armored SUV barreled forward, windows open and flashing lights ablaze. The people pushed and shoved to clear a path, and some cried out in pain. Alan echoed their cries, but his protest was cut short by the deadly gaze of the SUV driver. Then, with a flash of mutual recognition, he made eye contact with Keat Chhon sitting behind the driver. The SUV got past the crowd and roared away. Alan gaped; such a reckless action was completely out of character for Keat.

The ceremony was in shambles; children were crying, and the people spoke to each other in hushed, angry voices. Alan got his first aid kit and put on a tight dust mask to ward off the smells. He and Betty treated some minor injuries.

Betty asked, "Call the police?"

"That was the police."

Betty looked at the two injured children who needed more care than their first aid kit could provide. "Ambulance?"

Alan shrugged and pointed to his vehicle. He spoke briefly to the parents of the injured children, then gently lifted one of them. "Come on, we'll take them to the clinic." Betty followed Alan's lead and carried the other child to the Land Cruiser.

Gone Rogue

Harry Dunlap followed the paragliders through the border crossing into Cambodia. Well into his seedy sixties, Harry was an American secret agent, an old Asia hand. When Harry saw and recognized Alan, he slowed down, slunk to the side, and thought about how he could exploit the coincidence. Alan embraced a tall, blond, and attractive barang—*Must be Betty.* They loaded up his ancient vehicle and drove away.

Their spot was immediately filled by an expensive armored SUV. Keat Chhon, wearing an ornate, formal police uniform, waited in the backseat. Harry Dunlap approached and leaned down to the window.

"The eternal survivor, in the land of death," Harry said.

"Modern Cambodia—"

"Serving new masters, Keat?"

"I have always served the king."

"Another survivor." Harry nodded, got into the SUV, and put his bag on the floor. "Sorry, old comrades shouldn't quarrel."

They drove off through the increasing heat of the day and bullied their way through the traffic until they reached Koh Kong, where they approached an intersection jammed up by a bunch of monks clad in bright orange. Keat's driver, Sergeant Samphy—a burly, mean-looking Cambodian cop in a bush uniform—braked gently and slowed the vehicle.

"Turn on your siren and keep going," Harry said.

Samphy glanced at Keat's shocked face, but Harry's tone was stern and Samphy complied with Harry's orders. The crowd scattered as they pushed through, and Harry caught sight of Alan Grace. *He's obviously a magnet for trouble.* After they cleared the intersection, Harry looked through the back window at the angry crowd and thanked Samphy then turned to Keat. "See, no need to let superstitions slow us down." Keat's displeasure was clear, but Harry acted oblivious, looked him over, and said, "You've done well, Keat. Now we have business to discuss."

"Yes, agarwood," Keat acknowledged as his facial expression returned to neutral.

"Those fucking evergreen trees! Again."

"You liked them just fine when they helped you fund bin Laden," Keat replied.

"Yeah, like that worked out so well."

"The problem wasn't agarwood."

The problem was working with bin Laden, Harry thought, knowing that's exactly what Keat was thinking. This was one of the old wounds they shared. In the 1980s, Arabs had the biggest appetite (and the most money) for smuggled Cambodian agarwood. Under Harry's guidance, the CIA realized that agarwood oil (oud), with its strong Arabic connections, was an effective and clandestine way to fund al-Qaeda, their client in Afghanistan. Anything to beat the Russians in "the Great Game."

"Those trees," Keat said, "now generate half a billion dollars a year for Cambodia, and that's just the plantation products. Wild agarwood poaching is double that, at least."

Harry smiled. "Funny, we need samples, big ones, of exactly that: wild agarwood."

"It is possible. We could step up our efforts to … track smugglers and apprehend poachers."

Harry pulled a packet of banknotes half out of his bag and nodded at Keat's briefcase. When Keat opened the briefcase, Harry grinned, dropped the packet in, and said, "Uncle Sam still loves you." Then he ambushed Keat. "So, tell me about Alan Grace."

Harry could see that he had confused Keat—his question had

come on the heels of the recent sightings—but he only grinned harder and watched Keat get annoyed.

"Dr. Grace wrote the CITES clause to protect agarwood trees." CITES is the United Nations *Convention on International Trade in Endangered Species*. "And his plantation makes the best agarwood oil in Cambodia—"

"He's gone rogue, ducking charges back home."

Harry, the quintessential rogue, did not sway Keat. "Dr. Grace has promised to share his growing and distilling methods with the world."

"Why would he do that?"

"He's hoping to save what's left of the wild forests from the clear-cutters."

"How noble ... a good cover story."

Keat stared back.

"Come on, Keat, we've both outgrown our naive ideas."

Keat raised an eyebrow.

"We need to deal with him," Harry said; Keat remained unmoved.

"Grace is a threat!" Harry yelled.

Keat flinched and his cool demeanor started to melt. "A threat?"

Harry stared at Keat and leaned in until their noses were almost touching. He patted the briefcase with the cash. "Stay focused. Now it's Grace who is funding al-Qaeda."

"Grace is funding al-Qaeda?"

"He's an Arabist, very connected to Batar."

"The Bataris have never been implicated in terrorism," Keat

said, calm again.

"Nice Doctor Terrorist … we need to shut him down."

Keat stayed poker-faced, and Sgt. Samphy smiled.

Harry shrugged. "Let's go see his plantation."

"Now?" Harry had finally gotten to him.

"Yes, now. I saw him at the border this morning, and again just a minute ago, among all those monks. Why wait? We can get in and out before he even knows it." Harry pointed to Keat's phone. "Arrange for some backup to meet us there."

Samphy grinned and sped up.

Fat Sam's

Alan paid five US dollars, the medical fee to patch up the two kids, then they left the dimly lit clinic in Koh Kong. (The backpacker and tourist sites all said "Go to Thailand if you get sick," but the local people had no choice.)

"It's different from Thailand," said Betty.

"Koh Kong is a border town and a gambling destination for wealthy Thais. Believe it or not, it's an outpost of relative prosperity. By the way, no bank machines in the jungle. You need cash?"

"Yeah, haven't changed any money yet."

Alan laughed. "That's a good thing."

Betty got the joke after they drove to a bank machine and he pulled out $400. She blinked. "US dollars, not Cambodian riel?"

"You're in a failed state. Westerners and better-off Cambodians use US dollars. We use the riel for small change. Only the poor rely on the riel. That includes most of the population, but they don't have enough money to … to need dollars."

She got some dollars for herself, then they stopped in the middle of town at the (locally) famous Fat Sam's Restaurant: an open-air cement-floored hangout for Westerners, named after their most frequent customer, not the owner.

Alan ordered the cottage pie; he needed a break from Cambodian food before heading back into the mountains. On the other hand, Betty was eager to sample the local cuisine.

"Try the lok lak," Alan said.

Served on a bed of lettuce, tomatoes, and onions topped with cooked meat and smothered in a light gravy, it was delicious. Betty was an immediate convert. "I've just found my newest comfort food!"

Both hungry, they filled their faces and listened to the other customers exchanging expat and backpacker stories. After lunch, they headed up into the mountains to drive to Maran.

Betty first marveled at the lush mountainsides and the better-off settlements, then became quiet. She saw the poverty and garbage in many places and heard the sad history of the area, the last stand for Pol Pot and his band of Khmer Rouge murderers in the eighties. This road had been the last link in the supply chain for Chinese weapons coming through Thailand. The people suffered as the area changed hands several times between the Vietnamese and Pol Pot, each side in turn exacting punishment for collaboration.

They fell silent; she grew sleepy and drifted off…

Betty

Betty was lucky. She grew up in an enlightened household amid a caring California community. No one tried to curb her rowdy-girl tendencies even after puberty erased her body's androgyny and the ugly duckling turned into a beautiful swan. She was good at sports, wilderness camping, and most other physical pursuits. She also beat all the boys (and girls) at video games, then mastered all things digital by the age of fifteen.

Her early college admission—when she was only seventeen—was good because Betty took six years to complete her undergrad degree; she constantly switched her major. It wasn't dithering; there were just so many interesting things to discover in hard science, social science, the humanities, and the arts. The long, rambling undergrad years paid off; Betty had resolved the right-side/left-side brain conundrum that most people struggle with and was on her way to becoming a renaissance woman.

She'd had lovers, of course; the young men—and a few women—who'd had the courage to pursue her had given her pleasure, but no relationship had lasted. She was always very busy, and she'd found that pleasuring herself was more efficient and often more satisfying than navigating the dating scene. It was an old story: no one had captured her heart.

After a gap year of working and traveling, her plan to do her master's degree as a double major in biology and information technology made her the perfect candidate as Alan Grace's research and teaching assistant. They immediately hit it off and worked well together, almost as peers. She soon grew to love Alan (like a sweet older brother) and got swept up into his research and quest for improving domesticated agarwood.

Alan's singular focus on the biology of agarwood meant that he needed a lot of help in the ancillary areas, especially sorting out his data. Betty's contributions, based on her dual mastery of biology and computers, were key to integrating all the scattered progress he'd made over the years. With their lab on the brink of success, Alan declared that Betty was truly his mage.

Betty looked up the antique word, discovering that mage means magician or learned person. Perhaps Alan had bought into Arthur C. Clarke's third law: "Any sufficiently advanced technology is indistinguishable from magic."

Then Alan was called away to Cambodia to deal with his father's death. She ran his lab until the phony academic fraud charges and the raids shut it down. Bewildered by these events, she'd jumped at Alan's invitation to join him in Cambodia but not before she'd regained access to his data and done some other digital detective work.

Plantation Blues

Alan's Land Cruiser, splashing through muddy puddles, entered a poor village about four hours after leaving Koh Kong. Semi-naked children played in the puddles amid thatch-roofed hovels. Chickens ran about while the women worked together and the men chatted and smoked. Betty was agog. "What *year* is it here?"

"This is Maran." Alan stopped the vehicle.

"So poor."

"Better off than some. Many of them work at the plantation." Alan pointed past the village, across the river to the dense, steep hillside forest. "It's up there." Betty looked up to where Alan was pointing. "My father purchased everything from the river to that peak up there, and all the way over to the cliff at the other end."

"Cool," Betty said, untypically cryptic for a change.

Perhaps she was impressed? Alan continued. "The lab and the huts are just out of sight in the middle there, where you see a break in the trees."

An older villager approached them; it was Sakda. They got out and Alan reeled from the strong village smells, then recovered. He and Sakda exchanged wary, formal nods. "This is Sakda, our senior consultant and jungle expert, knows everything about agarwood. A great help … when we can find him." Alan grinned wryly, and Sakda shrugged. "He often disappears and pursues mysterious projects of his own."

Sakda seemed to ignore the innuendo. Always the handsome old gentleman, he grinned and greeted Betty with simple chivalry, then asked for a ride up to the plantation.

They all got in the Land Cruiser and drove to the rickety bridge and across the river. Alan worked the gas pedal and clutch as they lurched up the narrow, muddy, rutted track between the trees. Betty said, "Quite the commute!" She turned to address Sakda. "Such a steep hill. It looks like you have a long, hard walk to work."

"They sleep at the plantation most of the time," Alan said before Sakda could answer.

Betty glanced back and forth, then said, "Away from home?"

"From bed, yes. From home, no," Sakda said.

Alan squirmed. Betty pointed back down the road. "Isn't Maran your home?"

"Yes, but"—Sakda waved expansively at the forest—"all is Maran."

The vehicle wobbled; Alan steadied it. Sakda looked away, and they drove on in awkward silence until they came to the top, where they approached a clearing with some huts and a larger building. In big letters, a sign over the gate announced Grace Agarwood. Below it, a smaller inscription: Heaven's Scent.

"Heaven's Gate, eh? Where's St. Peter—" Betty's quip was punctuated by a gunshot.

They stopped; the gate was blocked by Keat's SUV. Another shot rang out from inside the gate. Betty gasped. "What the f—?"

"Shoot first, ask questions later." Alan shoved his video camera at her.

They ran through the gate while Sakda waited behind. Alan glanced back and saw him disappear down the road.

Betty started filming. Keat Chhon, Harry, Samphy, and a group of six soldiers confronted Leng and the other plantation workers. Between the two groups, a plantation worker lay dead; Sgt. Samphy had his handgun out, the obvious killer. Leng leapt at Samphy and was grabbed by the soldiers. Alan tried to intervene, but the soldiers blocked him, and Samphy hit Leng, hard.

Keat noticed that Betty was filming, and he signaled Samphy to stop. Alan turned. "Colonel! What is this?"

"Self-defense. We were attacked," Keat said.

"What are you doing here?"

"Police business." Keat was trying to hide his discomfort. "CITES inspection."

"CITES … you're not serious?" Alan grabbed Leng's hand and pulled him away from the soldiers.

"We suspect poachers are working here. We're investigating … convention violations."

"Come on, I wrote the convention. I'm—"

"We will compare your CITES licenses with the results of this inspection."

Alan shrugged. "You're wasting your time." Then he noticed the army truck parked near the lab. He shouted, "You took my computers?"

Harry spoke up. "We seized them as part of the investigation."

Alan looked at Harry, noticing him for the first time, and scowled. "Who are you?"

"US State Department," Harry said, casually belligerent. "Just helping out local law enforcement."

At Keat's gesture the soldiers returned to their truck and squeezed in among the computers while Samphy, Harry, and Keat got in the SUV. The two vehicles drove through the gate, maneuvered past Alan's Land Cruiser, bumped along, splashed through puddles, and drove away in a hurry. Alan looked at Leng. "What the hell?"

"Sorry, boss, we were out, busy with tree work. They come—"

"Not your fault," Alan said, much softer.

Betty said, "US State Department? I gotta get online."

Alan frowned, went to the dead worker, and shook his head. Though the strong scent of blood made him cringe, he knelt down, looked closely at his dead employee, then hung his head, further ashamed that he didn't even know the man's name. "We'll get him back to Maran ... and pay for the funeral." He was secretly relieved that the dead worker looked too young to have kids, which he confirmed with Leng.

He grieved quietly until Leng broke the silence. "They took everything. The oil—"

"The wild batch?" Alan asked, instantly alert. Leng nodded. Alan sagged. "Killing my workers. Taking my research, my data, the last of my wild oil. I'm royally screwed."

Betty pointed at her luggage. "Alan, I brought my own computers, all five. And I made sure that your data is safe." She pointed toward the buildings. "Come on, they didn't take the satellite dish."

Alan left Leng to deal with the workers and the dead body, then drove through the gate and over to the lab, a well-constructed building attached to a smaller annex. It was a hi-tech outpost in the jungle: a satellite dish, solar panels, a huge generator, and fuel storage tanks. Cables and pipes snaked everywhere and connected everything. It was set apart from the sleeping huts and a larger cookhouse.

Other workers emerged from the huts and trees, obviously relieved that the authorities had left, and they helped unload Betty's stuff while talking urgently among themselves.

Alan took Betty to the cookhouse. The shock of the raid was fading, and they were hungry after the long drive. "This is Tevy, Sakda's niece, Leng's mother. She's our cook." Tevy gave them each a warm greeting and a delicious fresh-baked baguette, the most useful French legacy still found in Cambodia.

Leng joined them, acknowledged his mother, and grabbed a baguette. "Where is Sakda?"

Betty looked around, shrugged. "Sakda rode up with us, but I haven't seen him since." Alan and Leng exchanged a look; they were used to his uncle's unpredictable behavior.

But, given the police raid, Sakda's disappearance was very predictable…

Sakda and Leng

Born on Cambodian Independence Day in 1953, Sakda grew up in Maran, a valley in the Cardamom Mountains where most people were oblivious to the modern political developments going on in Phnom Penh, less than two hundred kilometers away. Eventually Cambodian politics would greatly affect the area, but Sakda lived a happy if primitive life until his early twenties, when the Americans and North Vietnamese invaded Cambodia to battle each other. The invasions, and especially the American bombings, provoked the beginning of the civil war that eventually enabled the Khmer Rouge to take over. Then, the seemingly endless civil war spread to all corners of Cambodia, and the formerly forgotten Cardamom region eventually became a tattered battleground.

Being young, adventurous, and mostly unattached, Sakda headed west. He avoided the war, hunted agarwood, and then sold it to the Thai people in the border areas. He became adept at finding and using clandestine routes between Thailand and Cambodia. When the Vietnamese invaded in 1979 and the Khmer Rouge used the Cardamom as refuge and military base for their last stand, Sakda rescued friends and family and others. He smuggled them into Thailand where they lived in what were mislabeled as "Khmer Rouge refugee camps" and waited. The Khmer Rouge's last stand lasted a long and tragic decade due to the misguided international support they received against the Vietnamese.

Among the folks Sakda saved were his sister and her daughter, Tevy. He helped them resume life in Maran when the civil strife finally ended and was blessed with a grandnephew, Tevy's son Leng. Sakda did his best to teach Leng the lessons from his own childhood and to fully appreciate life in the valley and wild jungle nearby. Leng also learned much of Sakda's agarwood knowledge, which he later put to good use on the Grace plantation.

Leng and Alan had become good friends as teens when Alan had visited with his father. He had Alan's trust, had long ago been recognized for his abilities and the respect he had among the other workers, and his English was pretty good and getting better. When Alan took over the plantation, he promoted Leng to manager, part of a family tradition.

The Trader and the Hunter

Sakda entered a small hilltop clearing where a trail turned into a dirt road, two valleys over and a long drive from Maran. In the middle of the clearing stood Yuying Li (pronounced "Lee"), fiercely beautiful but dressed rough. "Hello, Wylie," Sakda said, using her famous nickname. She smiled broadly and returned the warm greeting. Yuying's bodyguard, Fan, watched from a few steps away—the few Khmer who knew her name mispronounced it as "Pan."

After seeing the raid at the Grace plantation, Sakda had immediately borrowed a smart phone. He wanted to get some good money for his remaining hoard of wild agarwood … before it was stolen. He contacted Yuying and arranged to meet her the very next day.

Sakda was a seasoned jungle trekker. He and a helper had taken hidden trails through the mountain passes, avoiding both the long drive and potential scrutiny on the roads. Ever cautious, Sakda had brought only a sample to the clearing; the main stash was a ways back in the forest, off the trail and guarded by his friend.

Sakda pulled a piece of dark wood from his bag and gave it to Yuying. Her nostrils flared, she smiled again, counted out five hundred dollars, and offered it to Sakda. Sakda gratefully accepted. "And for the main lot? Four thousand per kilo," she suggested. Sakda smiled and looked down. "Okay, five," she tried.

"Hard to find."

"I know. You're the best." Yuying took out her phone and got a picture of the wood piece. "I can go to six. No more."

Sakda nodded; she put the wood piece in her bag, then smiled and held the phone up to snap a picture of him. He grimaced and blocked his face with his hands. "No photo."

Yuying shrugged and put the phone away. "Okay. Meet here; three o'clock?"

Sakda smiled and agreed.

Fan drove Yuying down the hill to a crowded, primitive, open-air café that anchored a little village that was strung out along a paved road. The café sat on a corner where a dirt road came out of the jungle and down a steep hill behind the village. Yuying's jeep rolled down the hill and parked at the café. Yuying got out, leaving Fan behind the wheel, and entered the building, drawing stares from all around. She ignored the attention, looked for a free table, and was stunned to see Harry Dunlap sitting next to Sgt. Samphy. Harry was looking mean and chewing gum. "Do we believe in coincidence?" he asked.

"No, only bad karma," she replied.

Harry smiled, but Yuying did not return it. She had recently rebuffed him and his Cambodian police helpers, the first time they'd met. He'd tried to enlist her help to complete the collection of samples that he required. In addition to the oil that he'd stolen from Alan, he also needed some unprocessed wild agarwood.

"Relax, Yuying. What's up?"

"Nothing." She involuntarily clutched her bag, suddenly heavy with the precious wood. "None of your business."

She squirmed as Harry noticed the bag and her possessive reaction. "We should work together, my dear. I can save you time, make you rich." Yuying rolled her eyes and walked past Harry as he continued. "You don't know what you're doing. I have help..." She ignored him, shook off a bug that was crawling up her pant leg, and headed to the back of the café.

Yuying sat down at the table most distant from Harry and tried to figure out how he had known to follow her there. A tracking device on her vehicle perhaps? Outside, Keat Chhon's SUV and a police 4x4 came up the paved road and parked at the café. Keat and a tall, thin cop named Kosal got out and entered. Yuying recognized them from when she'd met Harry. People all around tensed up at the sight of the uniformed police, then gradually resumed more guarded conversations.

Harry acknowledged obsequious greetings from Kosal, then chatted with Keat. They glanced at Yuying as they spoke. She pretended to ignore them while checking her phone, but she was really taking photos. One of the onlookers joined their conversation. He looked at Yuying and then gestured up the dirt road while explaining something to Harry and Keat. Yuying squirmed but maintained her poker face as they got up, left the café, and got in their vehicles. Harry joined Keat; they turned left, back down the paved road. Yuying relaxed momentarily as she watched Harry and Keat heading away from her planned rendezvous. But when she saw that Samphy had joined Kosal, and that they had turned hard right into the dirt road and gone up the hill, she turned pale, her stomach in knots. She stayed in the café and watched the remaining cops set up their vehicle as a roadblock.

***

The two cops came round the bend and saw two men—their quarry—up the road at the clearing. Kosal goosed the gas pedal and steered the 4x4 directly at the older man. Samphy raised his rifle and took a shot. The older man dropped the water bottle, dodged bullets, and ran into the trees. Samphy fired at the other man. He went down. The 4x4 skidded to a stop next to the fallen man. Samphy jumped out and kicked the body, then dumped big pieces of dark agarwood from one of the bags. He rubbed on a piece, sniffed it, then smiled at Kosal. But Kosal was distracted by something and pointed at the brush. Samphy turned, saw a hat, and shot at it. It fell to the ground.

Kosal laughed and ran to the brush, but when he leaned in toward the fallen hat, a slipknot trapped his hand. He was pulled into the brush, and his hands were tied together. He called for help as he caught a glimpse of the old man disappearing into the trees.

Samphy walked cautiously over to the brush with his gun

drawn, checked very carefully around the area, then shushed up his partner and waited, listening intently. Finally, he knelt down, cursed Kosal, and untied him. But when he headed back to their 4x4, he screamed out loud and cursed again. The big bags of agarwood were gone.

Kosal screamed too, running over and uselessly brandishing his gun. A few scattered agarwood pieces remained next to the body that was already attracting ants. They looked around full of fear, then urgently gathered up the few remaining pieces and went back down the hill.

***

Yuying stopped picking at her food when Samphy's 4x4 roared back down the hill and stopped at the roadblock. She saw Samphy get out and pass around a piece of wood ... but no one looked happy. Soon, all the cops sped away down the paved road in the direction that Keat and Harry had gone.

Yuying jumped in her jeep and pointed Fan up the hill. When they pulled into the clearing and saw the body, she got out and turned it over. It was swarming with ants in the heat. At first she was puzzled and then relieved; it wasn't Sakda. Her relief turned to anger, then determination as she grabbed her phone and took photos. Even in the middle of the jungle, her phone pinged as the photos were sent to the cloud and added to her private online gallery.

Another dead hunter! And the best agarwood, so close and now gone. She cursed Harry and Keat...

Harry and Keat

Bad timing. Harry Dunlap had very bad timing, at least at the beginning of his career. With an honors degree focused on Southeast Asian history, and a head full of ideas about *making the world safe for democracy*, he'd applied to the Peace Corps. By the time Harry got interested, however, the Corps had been pretty well eclipsed by the US government's singular focus on the war in Vietnam. The savvy CIA agent vetting the new Peace Corps recruits had spotted him and soon convinced him he could be more effective working for a different branch of the government. He joined the CIA and did a full course of black ops training. He found some of the training difficult to reconcile with his idealism, but he decided to stay with the CIA. He was sure he could make a positive difference if he worked inside the system.

He arrived in Phnom Penh in 1975, a few weeks before the Khmer Rouge takeover. Harry soon fled Cambodia for the safety of South Vietnam only to arrive in Saigon the same week as the North Vietnamese. He'd reluctantly joined the humiliating exodus by helicopter from the roof of the US embassy.

In the chaotic aftermath, Harry was sent to work for the new Drug Enforcement Agency (DEA) office in Chiang Mai, northern Thailand. He chased drugs across Southeast Asia until he eventually confirmed his long-time suspicions that the biggest drug dealers were actually CIA fronts or partners.

He got himself transferred to the Defense Intelligence Agency (DIA) and liaised with the Thai military until Washington ignored his advice and picked the wrong side in a failed coup. Harry finally went back to the CIA who promptly dispatched him to Cambodia in the early 1980s where he found himself helping the bad guys—Washington and much of the international community were supporting the Khmer Rouge against the Vietnamese intervention. The remnants of Harry's moral compass were thoroughly extinguished when he was briefly trapped on the wrong side of a battle and killed some innocent villagers in a panic. He found out that taking a life, especially an innocent life, changed you forever … and not in a good way.

Abandoning his idealism, he became good at his job. Which effectively meant "America first," and screw the rest if they got in the way.

Then Harry's luck changed when he met and worked with Keat Chhon, a mercurial authority figure who always seemed to survive and thrive amid the factional ups and downs before, during, and after the Cambodian civil war. The chaotic situation allowed many to plunder Cambodian resources. Keat and Harry were particularly successful in acquiring and smuggling agarwood. They both got rich doing this but wisely hid their wealth from their respective masters.

Harry's career took off when he found a new use for the agarwood that was making him personally rich. He became a favored operative by smuggling agarwood to fund bin Laden in Afghanistan while keeping the CIA's role hidden.

Moving to the National Security Administration (NSA), he backed Keat Chhon in the transitions when the civil war finally ended. First, he made sure that Keat was the senior Cambodian in the security apparatus under UNTAC, the UN stewardship. Then, when the UN gave up and left the kleptocracy in power, Keat became the head cop for the renewed sovereign government.

Harry's detailed involvement in Cambodia gradually ended when he got promoted to a new, secret, multi-agency position—leader of all US clandestine activities in Southeast Asia. Harry's cover story had him working out of a small office in Bangkok as the US State Department trade envoy for the region. In his real position, he was reporting directly to the White House; it was a big job with immense power.

The White House had recently ordained that SpringenRx should receive all possible assistance from the US government as long as it was kept secret. Harry was used to solving his bosses' problems while maintaining the complete deniability of US connections. Like the fictional agents in *Mission Impossible*, he could count on almost unlimited covert backup but never a public defense if he were ever exposed.

Video Developments

Betty slowly got over her shocking arrival at the plantation. The police raid, the dead worker, and the grand theft of Alan's works had put her well beyond her comfort zone. She coped by getting right to work. After a couple of days, she even grinned a bit as she continued sorting out her tech gear in the lab annex and bopping along with the ska music blasting from her large, colorful headphones while the sun set outside the window. She wore a gritty fashion statement conjured up from a cheap T-shirt and Goodwill bargains. Two of her large travel bags sat open, with various computers and gadgets half unpacked, cluttering up the area. She was working at her giant computer screen when Alan entered from the main lab, stopped her personal soundtrack by yanking off her headphones, and demanded, "Where's my data?"

Betty's grin faded. She was annoyed, but that soon morphed into concern; she'd never seen Alan looking so glum. Guessing that he was still grieving his dead worker, she shrugged and went back to work on her keyboard where she entered a long string of characters.

"Fantasmarific!" Her sunny nature reemerged. "You are sooo lucky."

Alan looked baffled. She beckoned him to come and see her screen.

"I have duplicated and encrypted your data." He leaned in as she hit the enter key. "And hidden it on the web."

Betty's screen filled up with explicit porn pictures.

"You did what?"

"I hid it in pictures."

"In *porn*?"

"Its called 'digital steganography.'"

Medieval priests and spies had invented steganography when

they hid secret messages within intricate images. More recently, computer scientists had reinvented this practice as digital steganography—complex digital image files were the perfect medium in which to hide data. And impossible to decipher without the key. She scrolled the site. "Every image on *Debbie Does Dallas* has a few extra bits."

"Just a few!"

Betty turned serious. "Your data is safe. You can download it anywhere you can watch."

"In high def?" He shook his head. "Please just get me the data."

"Already downloaded."

"Great—"

"But reconstruction will take some time."

"Good luck finding all the little bits."

"Oh, and Mr. State Department? Good idea to get that on video. His name is Harry Dunlap; he's the Special Trade Envoy for Southeast Asia."

Alan frowned then smiled, and in a raised voice said, "CIA?"

"NSA?" Betty said, self-mockingly. Then she raised her pitch again. "Blackwater shadow ops!"

They laughed hard together.

"I expected better from Keat Chhon, though. He's been an ally, helped us out at times."

"Hard to resist the great USA."

"Maybe I should give this up. Never thought I'd cause a murder."

"You didn't cause the murder. You can't let the bad guys win."

"Win?" Alan asked.

Betty didn't like this version of Alan, so she switched the subject. "I'll reconstruct the data. In the meantime, I've set up my laptop with your video editing software, your work in progress, and all the raw video for your next documentary. It includes a bunch of video clips from Ken. Have a look at those first."

Alan perked up.

"And I even found some new photos for you, shared on Google. They're pretty gruesome, but based on what I saw when we arrived, they do make a point. This is way bigger than what happened here. We've got to tell the world."

She found his framed award and handed it to him. "Here's your Greenie. Go win another."

Alan took his award and walked through the large door from the annex into his lab. He went up to his "wall of fame"—a collection of degrees, awards, and photos—and removed a piece. He hung up the framed Greenie award, looked at the piece he'd removed, and shrugged. It showed him when he was much younger, soaring gloriously across the sky on a paraglider. Still on the wall was a montage of paragliding shots. He longed to go sailing again but had more urgent issues to resolve.

Alan felt bad about his curt behavior with Betty. The raid and killing, devastating in themselves, had also made the embargoed data from the university lab indispensable. He'd underestimated the challenge of setting up a functioning lab in the Cambodian jungle. Money wasn't a problem even though his father's estate was modest; King Kareem was a generous and enthusiastic backer of Alan's work. But it took months to find and import the right equipment and more months to do the work. Prior to the raid, he'd finally caught up and was close to a breakthrough. Now, his locally generated data, replicating what he had left behind at his university, had just been stolen. Access to his university data would keep him sane; he couldn't face repeating his work a third time. He decided he could wait for Betty.

In the meantime, Alan switched gears and went to work on the new documentary. He'd neglected to turn on the lights after sunset, and Betty's laptop glowed in the dark lab. He searched in the folder Documentary2 and found a clip labeled "Interview with Princess Nazneen." As always, his heart skipped a beat at the sight of her name. He started the video:

> Under a large poster, "Beauty World Asia IV," gorgeous models mingled and sampled fragrances. The view shifted to Nazneen, an attractive, regal, austere young Arab woman wearing her suit jacket with the collar done up and a hijab scarf over her head. Alan came on screen and said, "Your Highness, we hear that Dior, Ford, and Armani have started using agarwood oil in their perfumes."

> Nazneen laughed. "Christian, Tom, and Giorgio are agarwood latecomers."

> "They have competition?"

> "Arabs—in fact all Asians—have long revered agarwood's fragrant power." She held up three tiny vials. "Based on ancient formulas, Arabian Scents launched three new agarwood perfumes at this show. To fill growing demand, plantations thrive across Southeast Asia, fueling a ten-billion-dollar trade in domesticated agarwood."

Alan clicked to pause the playback and tagged the piece with a thumbs-up symbol for the post-production editor. But something was bugging him, an uncomfortable memory—they'd quarreled. He scrolled through and found a subfolder labeled "raw takes." It contained all the unedited video footage recorded at the show. He found and launched the clip that had been recorded just prior to Nazneen's interview:

The view jerked around before it settled and focused on Nazneen. Unlike her appearance in the formal interview, she looked casually beautiful and sexy. She was bareheaded with her hair loose; her jacket was off and hung over a chair, and her shirt collar was open.

An attractive blond camera-crew intern in T-shirt and shorts worked close behind while Nazneen read from a storyboard on a tablet computer.

Alan, offscreen and voice only, said, "Okay, let's get you wired up." He came into view, dug into an equipment bag, pulled out a microphone, and pinned it on Nazneen.

Behind them, the intern's cord snagged, and her light stand tottered. Alan pivoted over and deftly caught it just in time. He freed the cord and grinned at the intern, who promptly flushed. Alan started to sway; he stopped himself with a headshake.

Nazneen noticed and tried to hide her annoyance by reading the tablet. Then something in the storyboard agitated her. "You want to start with the aphrodisiac angle?"

"It's a great hook for the story," he said.

"But I don't have your deep expertise."

"You started it," he said.

"Are you talking about … I was nine years

old!"

"So was I."

They locked eyes with their faces full of confused emotion. Alan blinked first, shrugged, and looked away. He took the tablet from Nazneen and reviewed the script. "Okay, we'll find a different way into the narrative." He swiped through several pages looking for the right topic. "Gotta grab the viewer's attention."

"Use the Garden of Eden story again?"

Alan shook his head, swiped to another page.

"The clear-cuts?" Nazneen asked.

Alan stopped, moved closer to Nazneen, and pointed to the tablet. As she angled it to see it better, it got picked up by the video camera and showed a photo of a dead hunter with the caption "Accused Poacher Killed by Cops."

"No," Alan said, "I'll start this one with the murder story."

Suddenly, an instant message from Betty popped up over the scene.

- I'm done.

Alan stopped the video but failed to answer Betty.

Betty yelled out, "Your data? It's ready."

She entered from the annex and held up a small USB key fob. The fob had a distinct logo: OPAL. "I've linked everything to this uncloneable key." She went to the laptop and plugged the key fob into the side. A new image appeared on the screen: OPAL Defender. When Betty clicked, the program demanded security verification. "It has a small fingerprint scanner. Put your thumb there."

Alan put his thumb on the fob. A chime sounded, the screen refreshed and said, "Print Locked."

Betty pulled the fob out of the laptop, held it up. "Don't lose this. Even I would have trouble accessing your data without it."

Alan took the fob, stared at it, and stuck it in his pocket. He was still thinking about Nazneen...

Alan and Nazneen

Batar, Arabian Gulf, 1993

Nine-year-old Alan Grace looked fondly up at his father, David, inhaling that leather smell of luxury in the back of the big limo as it passed through tall, swaying palms and entered the Batari Royal Palace courtyard. (Alan's father was the Batari royal family's business manager. Alan had been spending his school vacation with his dad, when an urgent situation in Batar had required a sudden business trip to the small Arabian Gulf kingdom.) When the limo door opened, another scent—new but somehow achingly familiar—assaulted Alan's olfactory glands, and his nostrils flared.

A little dazed, Alan endured the formal greetings with King Kareem and was then introduced to his beautiful young daughter, Princess Nazneen. She called him "Alangrace," saying his name sweetly as a single word. He happily followed her to the playroom, off the main hall of the palace, while Kareem and David went into the palace office at the opposite end of the hall.

In the playroom, the children giggled at the sleeping, comically snoring governess. They abandoned their board game, crept out, and made their way upstairs to the late queen's boudoir. Alan was awed by the sheer luxury and the sumptuous array of fancy fragrance bottles.

Nazneen said, "Let's play house." Alan nodded. "Okay, I'll be the queen and you can be the king."

"You said play *house*." Alan went rigid.

"This is my house. I'm a princess, you know!"

Alan couldn't reconcile the defiant girl in front of him with his image of a princess but soon became engrossed in the game. Nazneen draped beautiful silk shawls over her clothes and walked around in oversized high heels while Alan pretended to be regal and aloof.

Nazneen found a perfume bottle. "The queen requires her

fragrance." She sprayed it, and it sent Alan into a swoon.

Nazneen kissed Alan on the lips; he stared back at her, alarmed and alert.

Kareem came into the room, not pleased with the mess. "Clean up," he said to Nazneen. He escorted Alan back down to the main palace hall.

Kareem picked up a dark wood chip and threw it on a brass brazier filled with burning charcoal. Alan surprised Kareem. He recognized the scent from the burning agarwood chip and even connected it with the perfume that had recently slayed him. "Maybe you are destined to follow the Scent of Heaven," Kareem said with a knowing smile and a twinkle in his eye. He motioned for Alan to sit on the big sofa.

Alan sat down and looked ahead without focusing. The smoky aroma of the burning chip swirled about his head. It reminded him again of the fragrance in the bedroom and provoked images of Nazneen's pretty face. Strong feelings, the kind that stayed with you your whole life.

Nazneen came cautiously down the stairs and after a forgiving nod from her father joined them on the sofa. Sitting deliberately between them, Kareem further explained this powerful scent called oud, the Arab name for agarwood. He fetched several big picture books to help tell the story, much of which is shrouded in mythology and religion. Kareem used the beautiful images from the books and told the story in a fairy-tale style to hold them spellbound. This was what they learned…

Agarwood was praised in the Sanskrit Vedas from India, one of the world's oldest written texts, and played a role in the western creation myth when Adam and Eve were allowed to take only this one plant from the Garden of Eden.

Sheba and Solomon used oud to seduce each other in ancient Arabia—in Batar itself, according to local myth. It often served as a traditional medicine in many places. Even the famous place name Hong Kong translated literally to "Fragrant Harbor," named for the incense trees growing on the hillsides around the harbor. Like their ancestors, many people today still burned agarwood chips or incense as a spiritual offering and meditation aid. And agarwood oil had become the key ingredient in famous European, Arabian, and Asian Perfumes.

Story time was over, but the children were still glued to the picture books when David Grace left the palace office and joined them in the main hall. Kareem teased him. "At least one of you infidels shows some appreciation for the more important things in life."

David didn't get it.

"Your son seems to love agarwood, like an Arab. Knows value, not cost."

"I know both." David had the opening he needed. He and Kareem had been discussing the growing cost of agarwood and its impact on the Batari treasury. This was one of the issues that had prompted the unplanned visit to Batar. David had given advice on how to immediately boost cash reserves but had held back on his idea for a comprehensive resolution. Now he proposed his longer-term fix for the depleted treasury: the purchase of land in Cambodia for future agarwood plantations. Cambodia was both the source country for some of the best agarwood and a barely recovering failed state that welcomed almost any form of foreign investment. Kareem was immediately intrigued by the proposal and wanted to know more.

When the adults finished their discussion and the seminal visit to the palace ended, King Kareem gave Alan a small Chinese agarwood carving and said, "I want you to have this … the first piece of a fine collection, I'm sure. Alan Grace: Agarwood Hunter!"

Lab Work

Alan bathed in the bright morning sun that streamed through the lab windows, worked intently at a microscope, and took notes. He wore a stained, frayed lab coat and looked rough after a series of all-nighters. When the bio-catalyzer beeped, he opened a panel on the big machine and exchanged a half-full beaker with an empty one.

Betty came in to check on things; she'd brought him a cup of coffee.

Alan grinned at her. "Finally, some progress."

"The data structure I designed … it fits okay?"

"Like a glove."

"Awesome."

"You solved my data problem," he said. "But for the final stage, I still need more wild oil."

"Hey, I noticed something weird in my data," Betty said.

"*Your* data?" Alan said.

Long used to Alan's self-centered myopia, Betty rolled her eyes and got a small apologetic nod from Alan.

She carried on. "I hid a tracking program in the project files after they were embargoed." She scowled. "After they cut off our access, they let the FDA in. They copied everything."

"The FDA, SpringenRx…" Alan mused.

"So, I had a peek at the FDA server."

"You hacked the FDA?" What's next, the Pentagon?

"SpringenRx has secured a bunch of approvals for new drugs. Get this—they're based on synthesized agarwood molecules."

Alan frowned, then nodded. "Agarwood was used as a

traditional medicine … in ancient times, before it was an export commodity."

"Before it cost a hundred thousand per liter, you mean."

"Correct. I guess SpringenRx could charge a small fortune for their synthetic agarwood drugs … and still beat that price."

"And they claim it'll cure a ton of diseases, even tumors."

It was like someone turned on a light. "That's why SpringenRx wants to shut me down."

"Exactly. If you succeed, anyone can grow good agarwood."

"And no one will need their expensive synthetic version."

Calling Arabia

Much later in the again-darkened lab, Alan opened a Skype-like program, IronChat~Secure Communications, and clicked on a tiny photo of the Batari Royal Palace, the call button for King Kareem. Kareem soon answered and appeared onscreen in the palace's main hall, amid exotic plants and next to wood chips burning on a charcoal brazier. Before Alan could become nostalgic, he noticed that Kareem was troubled. "Your Highness, what's wrong?"

"Fallout poisoning from depleted uranium. Batar has a new disease."

"Fallout? Depleted uranium?" Alan asked.

"Used in the war."

"Which war?"

"The George Bush war."

"Which George Bush?"

"Take your pick," snapped Kareem, uncharacteristically harsh.

Alan struggled to open his mouth and failed.

Kareem toned down. "Actually it was Bush One. What your people called the 'Gulf War.' Hmm. Your people often forget what they have done to … to … *to help Arabs*."

"I don't know what to say." Alan was gobsmacked, but he recovered. "But Batar wasn't bombed."

"We are downwind. We have over fifty people, critically ill."

Alan shook his head trying to get his mind around this; he knew Batar, and many Bataris, well. Kareem shrugged and moved on. "Nazneen sends her regards. And asks about your research."

"Its coming along. I—" Alan flashed to his storybook lesson years ago and connected it to his very recent talk with Betty. "Wait, your perfumery, does it have a good supply of oud?"

"Of course. *You* need some?"

"It's crazy expensive, but you could try the oil as a treatment. The old myth…"

"About using the oil as medicine?" Kareem raised his eyebrows.

"Might have some basis in truth."

Kareem nodded. "All the conventional treatments are failing."

"The cost will be off the charts."

"What's the price of a life?" Kareem was newly energized. "We'll try it."

PING, PING. A text message popped up on Alan's screen:

- Dr. Grace, re: amazing wild agarwood sample. Please meet me. Tomorrow 7pm Sora Bar Vattanac Tower PP. Regards Y. Li.

Kareem heard the ping and noted Alan's interest. "You're busy. Stay in touch, Alan." He clicked off as Alan waved.

Alan puzzled out the message. "Y. Li," he said out loud, then laughed. For years he'd heard about *Wylie*, a legendary beautiful if elusive oud expert. Perhaps this invitation was a joke? Or had he heard the name wrong all this time—a Khmer accent on an Arab version of a Chinese name?

The prospect of meeting the famous, mysterious Wylie was … irresistible in any case, even if it took him a whole day to drive to Phnom Penh. With all due modesty, Alan considered himself the world's leading agarwood expert. He was anxious to meet anyone who might challenge that conceit…

Yuying

Yunnan, China, 1995

A young girl looked fondly up at her father, Heng, holding his hand as they wound through the narrow streets of the little village outside Jinghong. Yuying Li was precious to Heng, despite her birth being the cause of his wife's death. Perhaps he doted on his only child, but he never indulged her; she was no *little empress* like many of her one-child cohort. She grew up in his arms and now lived by his side as he struggled to make a living trading with the rough men who plied the Mekong River.

The Mekong flows through or touches seven different countries, from its source forty-five hundred meters high in Tibet to the wide delta entering the South China Sea, forty-five hundred kilometers later. It is the twelfth longest river in the world, the world's largest inland fishery, and second only to the Amazon for its biodiversity. Other great rivers, like the Amazon, the Yangtze, and the Mississippi, provided a navigable route deep into South America, Central China, and North America respectively. Not the Mekong. It was cut in two, and navigation was blocked by the escarpment at Khone Phapheng Falls in Laos. Enterprising French colonists failed in their attempt to build a portage railroad around the falls. This barrier left much of Southeast Asia and Southern China a provincial backwater region.

Still, the Mekong had long been an important if somewhat inefficient trade route for the local people. At the same time, it had also been a contested border and both the source of and avenue for conflict. The traders worked both above and below the falls. When they went north, they usually called in at Jinghong, the first big town on the Mekong in Yunnan, China.

Yuying shadowed Heng day by day and learned all about agarwood trading. At Heng's insistence, the traders brought live agarwood seedlings along with the precious wood pieces and refined oil. Heng knew that the agarwood trade was getting harder and harder for the small traders. He was determined to grow it in Yunnan, on a plantation, just like people in Cambodia, Laos, and most of Southeast Asia were starting to do. Yuying and Heng learned together about nurturing domesticated agarwood trees as they created a plantation.

The plantation was sanctioned as an official agricultural development policy and provided some cover for Heng's trading activities, which had been underground and secretive ever since a local party official had denounced him as a capitalist. However, the political support to get the land and organize the workers had attracted the attention of the triads, who were always expanding, even in the People's Republic. Agarwood, especially wild agarwood, became more valuable than their usual contraband—jewelry, drugs, and people—and the agarwood trade became more difficult and dangerous.

Jinghong, with its share of thuggery, was a typical Mekong trading town, but it was usually possible to avoid this side of things. Heng often brought Yuying with him to work, originally as child care, then more and more as a precocious assistant. She kept the books, did his paperwork, and even occasionally opined on the trades. On the day after her tenth birthday, they went together, down to the docks to do some business. Unfortunately, Heng had underestimated the triad's interest in his activities.

Yuying watched Heng greet three unfamiliar—and *ugly*— traders. It was a new connection that promised to be lucrative. These men seemed rough and nervous, and they ignored Yuying as she cringed behind her father, sensing that something was not right. Most of the traders that Heng dealt with were foreigners from downriver; these men definitely were not. She guessed that they were Chinese, but not locals, as she didn't recognize their dialect nor understand what was being said. Heng tried to end the dialogue and backed away abruptly, but the men were insistent. After more gruff words, Heng finally agreed to something.

Heng led Yuying away and took her to the school in their village. She was not pleased. Way ahead of her peers, she often out-thought the teacher and felt like a fish out of water. Heng insisted she join the class that day and left her singing patriotic songs with her classmates.

Yuying sang along then made quick work of her arithmetic exercise. Excused to use the privy, she soon snuck out of school and went back to the Jinghong docks where she kept out of sight to conceal her delinquency.

Heng was dealing with the strange men, and their negotiation turned nasty as she watched. One of the men pulled out a knife and stabbed Heng. Yuying screamed and ran to Heng; the men ransacked his pockets then jumped in their long-tail boat and took off up the river.

People nearby ran to the docks at the sound of Yuying's loud cries. She hugged and kissed her dying father and pointed at the disappearing fugitives on the river. They shouted at other boaters, but the mysterious men were long gone. They pulled her off Heng's body and carried her away from the scene of devastation. She stopped crying, fixed her stare on the distant boat, and vowed revenge.

***

The village didn't know quite what to do with Yuying. She was beautiful, determined, and already smarter than most of them. There were no volunteers to adopt her; she just carried on. In the end, they watched out for her but left her pretty much alone. She managed to keep the family home and the small, hidden fortune her father had earned.

Yuying worked on the plantation and befriended a big, tough older girl, appropriately named Fan (*Fan* means dangerous or lethal). She seemed especially attentive at keeping Yuying safe.

Yuying fed and then started paying Fan, who had become her bodyguard and surrogate family. They acquired weapons, both discreet and more obvious, and practiced with each other until they were a tight team. Only then did Yuying resume trading agarwood, using as seed money a small part of the secret stake Heng had left her. She had some success and earned some cash from trading but soon realized that it was her expertise she could more lucratively sell to the bigger traders. Her agarwood consulting paid very well, and her reputation spread as she became known for her unerring eye and nose, and the ability to translate that into market prices.

By the age of sixteen she'd been from Bangkok to Beijing and Baghdad. She celebrated her eighteenth birthday at the Musée d'Orsay in Paris then took college courses for half a year in Toronto. Somehow, she was never too long away from home base, her rebuilt house, and the local agarwood plantation nearby.

Her need for revenge, or rather the type of revenge, changed as she matured. When she figured out which triad group had killed her father, she laid traps for the kingpins and then used the anti-corruption squads, and the other law-and-order mechanisms emerging in China, to destroy them and their organization.

Eventually, Yuying spent most of her time closer to home. She watched in amazement as Jinghong grew, encompassed her village, and became a southern escape for the northern Chinese. It was a green, clean, unspoiled destination for the urban moneyed class who fled industrial disaster zones—the places they'd created to conjure up their wealth.

Yuying still occasionally visited global hot spots, and glamour definitely had its attractions when she morphed into a sophisticated beauty. But these pleasures paled in comparison to the thrill she felt when she traded directly with jungle hunters and brought home treasures. She loved to travel across Southeast Asia with Fan, hunting for agarwood in Thailand, Malaysia, Laos, and Cambodia.

Principles I

Alan nursed his beer and relaxed on the deck of the Sora Bar, thirty-seven stories high in the sky. He was tired after the long drive to Phnom Penh, and he was enjoying the break from his jungle habitat. An attractive waitress serviced the customers—a beautiful, well-dressed, mixed-race group of people, who toyed with their exotic cuisine. They were not concerned with the sweaty inhabitants of the streets far below. The bar was part of the Rosewood Hotel, which occupied the top floors of the stunning new Vattanac Capital Tower.

Alan got up, peered over the railing, and saw the Mekong pushing water into the Tonlé Sap River on the west side of Phnom Penh. The Tonlé Sap River reverses flow twice per year. Six months of the year it flows south into the Mekong, draining and shrinking the Tonlé Sap Lake. The other six months of the year, the relentless abundance of water from the mighty Mekong during rainy season pushes the water north and refills the huge shallow lake.

Alan turned and looked back at the two stories of cascading glass forming the sloping roof next to the deck; the architects in Asia were really stretching the limits, creating exciting buildings. Then he noticed a strong, pleasant updraft cooling the hot, humid evening.

Yuying Li, her fierce beauty softened and enhanced by a knockout red dress with matching fingernails and heels, came out of the hotel lobby and across the deck, attracting leers from the men and admiring stares from the women. She stopped at Alan's table and extended her hand. "Doctor Grace, so pleased."

Alan shook her hand and noticed her pleasing scent. He had to steady himself when she didn't let go of his hand.

"Sorry," she said and finally let go. "Yuying Li. I sent you that message."

"So the famous Wylie … oh, I mean *Y. Li*. What's up with your agarwood?"

"I have the sample, as promised. But … last year, at the UN conference? I heard you speak."

"Yes?" Alan remained skeptical.

Yuying sat down very close to him, almost touching. His nostrils flared at her strong, appealing fragrance. She smiled warmly. "Sir, we need your assistance."

Alan finally surrendered to her scent and her beauty; he loosened up and smiled. "We?"

"The Yunnan Agricultural Collective. We're having problems on our agarwood plantation." She took out her phone, put it on the table, then tapped and swiped it to show photos as she spoke. "We have a large plantation, but the quality of our oil is not consistently high."

Alan tapped on an image that caught his interest. Both of them alternately tapped and stroked the phone to punctuate their conversation and view certain images. Alan asked, "Which species?"

"Both, actually. The *Aquilaria* does a little better; we're a long way north of here."

Alan shrugged. "Well, sure, the tree thrives, but not the mold."

"We compensate using promiscuous applications."

"Some of the molds are swingers?" Alan said. They drew closer and accidentally touched as they continued stroking the phone.

"It can get pretty kinky."

Alan leaned back. "Which infection protocol?"

"Fast insertion."

"Limiting factor?" He leaned forward.

Yuying shook her head. "Full penetration."

"Climax?"

"Rarely."

Nose to nose, he was barely able to resist a kiss. He leaned away and sighed. "So, no climax infection, no agarwood. Okay, what elevation are you growing at?"

***

They were pretty much alone on the deck. It was late, but Alan hadn't noticed the time fly by. Yuying used her long red fingernail to scratch at a dark wood chip she pulled out of her purse. The aroma she released was almost visible as it engulfed them, and they both succumbed. Yuying recovered first. "My people say that one must live three righteous lifetimes before encountering pure agarwood."

Alan laughed. "I just proved them wrong."

"And then eight more lifetimes of merit before one can use and appreciate it."

"Which is ancient Chinese for *extremely rare*."

They laughed, eyes locked on each other, animal attraction surging on shared passion and knowledge of all things agarwood.

"I have access to more," Yuying said, breaking the spell.

"Slow down," he said, again wary. He held up his hands. "I can't get involved—"

"And I need your help."

"I've already got my hands full. Right here."

"At least consider it, you owe me that much."

"I owe you?" Alan was completely taken aback.

"You used my photos in your documentary!" When he didn't get it, she continued. "The smuggled pieces going to China? The murder victims?"

Alan got it. He hesitated as it sunk in. "Those photos are yours?"

Yuying nodded.

Alan recovered and pushed back. "My data analyst sourced those…" He hesitated again. "From a photo-sharing site?"

Yuying clobbered him. "Pfft. A password-protected private site."

Chagrined, Alan muttered to himself. "Betty."

Yuying took his hand and rubbed his fingers on the chip. He inhaled deeply and relaxed, then took the chip. "This is very fine. From the forest floor, no doubt."

"No, it came from a living tree."

Alan was impressed, if not convinced. Then he became suspicious. "The source?"

"Old hunters!" She was firm. "Traditional hunters, like my photos. Not clear-cutters, I promise … Alan, I have a proposition." He was alert and skeptical as she continued. "I may have access to several kilos of this."

Alan was alarmed. "What—?"

"If I can get it." She held up her hand. "I'll need an origin certificate and export license to ship it through Phnom Penh. Thanks to your convention, I can't use the Mekong riverboats—"

"Without the convention? Not a forest left in Cambodia! So what do you want?"

"To disguise my stuff. Get an origin certificate from you and export it as Grace Agarwood."

"Risking my reputation."

"I know about your research and the recent raid on your lab."

Alan was alarmed. "How do y—?"

"You need some of this." She opened a tiny vial of oil. To their sensitive expert noses, the strong aroma was certainly that of wild oud.

Alan waved it off. "I don't need your oil. I have … legitimate sources."

Yuying shrugged. "In theory. Alan, please, help me. You can have it all: the money, the oil and…" She grinned seductively. "Who knows where this could go?"

Alan ignored the flirting. "I can't take the risk," he said. Then he mocked radio headlines. "Today's top story: 'Treaty Writer Breaks Own Treaty.'"

Yuying took the vial and rubbed some oil on Alan's forehead.

He fought off a swoon, and his voice broke. "It goes against all my principles … everything I've worked for." His voice strengthened. "I can't help you."

Yuying turned her back. Face set, determined, she grabbed her stuff and stalked off the deck.

Principles II

Alan came back, but said nothing about his quick trip to the capital. Something was bothering him as he walked with Betty between tall trees in the farthest corner of the plantation. They checked tags and infection sites on the larger tree trunks while Alan sniffed at these spots and made video clips with small commentaries.

PING. Betty's phone had found a data signal.

"Hey!" She started poking at her phone. "There's a good signal here. Can't get internet access back at the lab without the satellite."

"That's 'cause we're over the hill here, at the top of the next big valley. That's the data stream for Xanadu." Alan went on to explain about the backpacker party-hut scene, located up the river and known as Xanadu. The cell companies, who made great profits from tourist SIM cards, had made sure that the barang backpackers got good data access, even at their remote jungle playground.

They walked a little farther before Betty broached a painful subject. "Sakda tells amazing stories."

Alan stopped and imitated Sakda. "All is Maran," he said and waved at the hillside.

Betty was not impressed. "I did some research. Your father purchased this land twenty-five years ago."

"He was setting up the Batari plantation. Found this one for himself … for his family, for me."

Betty nodded. "All good, 'cept this *was* all Maran territory. The village, the valley, and the hillsides. The government had no right to sell the land."

"My father was a good man!"

"True, they loved David Grace, even Sakda. But, bottom line: he bought stolen land."

"But the ... oh, forget it." Alan looked hurt. He walked toward the next tree and examined the tag.

Betty followed him. "Sorry, hate to ruin your day."

"Too late for that ... I can't do the assay test matching until I find more wild oil. It's like target practice. You have to know what you're aiming for. And my extraction permit to harvest wild agarwood expired. My own fault; I wrote a tight-ass convention."

"Retentive." Betty laughed. "But we can get ... creative!" She headed off, leaving Alan checking tags and sniffing trees.

***

Alan was still looking glum and working alone on a tree when Betty returned with Leng in tow. She tried sympathy. "That bad, eh?"

Alan ignored her.

"Boss, I haven't asked you for much." She got his attention. "Please trust me. Come with Leng and me. I want to introduce you to a real agarwood hunter."

Alan wanted to know more, but Betty corralled him and Leng into the old Land Cruiser. They drove down the hill to Maran, crossed the bridge, and parked next to a hut. Leng led them inside where they found Sakda hard at work, hacking dark wood chips from the core of a bigger piece. One of the chips smoldered in the small fireplace, filling the hut with a lovely aroma. Unlike the houses of affluent Southeast Asians, filled with cloying images of religion and royalty, the only images hanging on the walls of the primitive hut were the two saints of the worldwide underclass: Bob Marley and Che Guevara.

Alan and Sakda greeted each other skeptically before they all sat down. Alan didn't think much of this surprise and was about to complain when he was briefly overcome by the scents from the fireplace combined with the freshly trimmed wood.

Before the encounter went wrong, Betty broke the ice. "Hey. I'll bet you didn't know that the best agarwood hunter in Cambodia lives … right under your nose, so to speak." They shared a good laugh; Alan's amazing and sometimes crippling sense of smell was well known to all.

"Old agarwood, hard to find," Sakda said.

"I know." Alan nodded.

Sakda asserted himself. "Sakda find *one tree*."

"The convention forbids—"

"Like treasure hunt," Leng said. "No clear-cuts. Sakda find one tree. Very old, full with agarwood. He knows how to see inside. Take the one tree, leave forest."

"Maran people trust you?" Sakda abruptly changed the subject.

Alan was not sure whether to be puzzled or offended. "What? Excuse me?"

Leng intervened again and admonished Sakda with a "Don't be a cranky old man" look, then spoke to Alan. "Forgive Sakda. Again. Police, government, are bad, like bandits. Sometimes more bad." Then he turned back to Sakda and defended Alan. "He made me the boss man."

Sakda nodded and took a new, much darker chip from his pocket. "Our treasure." He rubbed it, then gave it to Alan.

"Wow!" Alan was startled by the strength of the fragrance and struggled again to stay in control as he rubbed on the wood and closed his eyes. "Do you have more of this?" he asked, forgetting all about CITES issues in the moment.

"All gone," Sakda replied. "But no good price."

Alan was puzzled; Leng intervened. "Before, Sakda made deal with Wylie. Got good price. But the police come, try to steal the agarwood. They killed Sakda's partner. No deal."

Betty reminded Alan. "Those new photos I downloaded for you."

Alan groaned and stared briefly at Betty, remembering the awkward moment at the Sora Bar regarding the photos that he'd used in his first documentary.

Then he looked at Sakda with new respect. His theoretical, generalized sympathies toward the poor folks who scratched a living in the Cambodian wilds had to be expanded to include this heretofore annoying villager and intermittent plantation employee. And to top it all off, Sakda had known Wylie, long before he himself had.

"Need money. Sakda sell, bad trader, low price," Sakda said.

Alan was used to mentally filling in the blanks and fixing grammar to discern the limited English of his workers. So, Sakda had been getting good prices for his wild agarwood by trading with Yuying Li until the crooked cops had intervened. He'd then been forced to sell to the double-dealing middlemen who paid low prices and sometimes even betrayed their suppliers to the police.

"All gone." Sakda repeated himself. Then he held his hand up. "Sakda find more. Find one tree. Sakda need help." He'd found an infected tree, especially full of agarwood, and he needed help to harvest it.

"Please help," Leng said. He lowered his voice. "Hide our treasure, like Grace Agarwood. Get good price, no bandits."

Alan couldn't believe he was hearing the same request again, so soon. "I can't … the treaty—"

"Maran needs a lot of money," Betty said. Money to fix the road that alternated between dust and mud, money to replace the leaky thatched roofs, and money to address the complete lack of local medicine or formal education.

Sakda reached out, held Alan's shoulder. "You. Come."

Alan was puzzled.

"Yes. Come to the jungle. See with Alan eyes," Leng said.

"Firsthand data samples," Alan said to no one.

Leng encouraged him. "Help Maran. Keep some treasure, finish your research."

Alan sniffed and rubbed the chip. "This is amazing."

Leng and Sakda smiled and nodded enthusiastically.

Alan held up his hands to stop them, handed the chip back to Sakda, and said, "I'm not promising anything. I need to…"

Betty joined the victory celebration and grinned as Leng and Sakda smiled even wider and held their thumbs up. But Alan pushed back one last time. "I'll … do a … feasibility study and get back to you."

"Feasibility study?" Betty said. "Sounds like academic politics."

Sakda rubbed on the chip, then gave it back to Alan.

He inhaled the scent. *Time to call Kareem.*

"I may have a buyer."

Principles III – Decision Time

They returned to the plantation. Alan went directly to his lab, double-checked the time difference for the Arabian Gulf, then got in touch with King Kareem via IronChat. He held up Sakda's chip. "I'm really torn about this, shouldn't have got involved … but high seven figures, maybe more! You interested?"

"Oh yes, desperately," Kareem said.

That got Alan's full attention. The king looked distraught. Alan had been so caught up in his own predicament that he hadn't noticed.

"You were right. An effective treatment for the Gulf War disease," Kareem said.

"Good news!"

"Yes, but I have some bad news. The disease is very … *democratic*. Royalty is not immune." Kareem shifted his cam. Nazneen was still beautiful but frail and bedridden. Kareem added, "Quite sudden."

"Hello, Alangrace," Nazneen said softly, reverting to her childhood version of his name.

Alan gaped. "I would've come, if I'd known."

"Of course, but your work there is more important. Especially now," Kareem said.

Across the screens and the many miles, Alan and Nazneen silently reconnected. "I'm sorry," he said.

Kareem gave them a moment, then said, "And you offer us a real treasure, an immediate lifesaver! We need it, whatever the price."

"And Maran desperately needs the money," Alan said.

"I'll send my plane."

"Not yet," Alan said and got puzzled looks from Kareem and

Nazneen. "We have to go get it first." Kareem's look turned skeptical; Nazneen looked worried. "Sakda knows where it is."

"You're not going into the jungle?" Kareem said.

"Yourself?" Nazneen said, almost talking over her father.

Alan nodded.

"Risky," Kareem said. "Why?" asked Nazneen at the same time.

"Scientific curiosity?"

"My fault," Kareem said. "Filling your young head full of fables."

"I'll be okay. I just need to know if you're committed?"

Kareem nodded. "We'll arrange a little entertainment in Phnom Penh, to distract the inspectors." Kareem's phone rang, and he waved goodbye as he left the room to answer it.

Alan and Nazneen looked at each other.

"Hang on. I'll get it for you. I promise."

Getting In

 Now that Alan had decided to sponsor and join the hunt, he was eager
to get started. They found an eco-tour operator who was delighted to
sell his kayaks for a handsome profit. Leng recruited three of the
plantation workers to join the expedition, and they packed for a quick
trip into the jungle. Two days after his promise to Nazneen, Alan
figured that while they were ready for anything, it was likely going to
be a relaxing weekend getaway.

 Early in the morning, next to the Maran village bridge, six men
loaded and launched three large kayaks. They waved goodbye to Betty
who was dressed in a sort of camouflage: baggy sweatpants and a
hoodie. She got in Alan's Land Cruiser, drove through Maran and
away from the plantation and the river.

 Leng, Sakda, and Alan set off and paddled upriver, each
piloting a kayak. Alan wore a utility vest over his life jacket rigged
with a sports cam and a small solar panel. An hour into their journey,
they came around a bend and then passed a high cliff on one side of
the river. The Xanadu party huts, ramshackle buildings with large
decks, sat atop the cliff. Despite the early hour, the parties were in full
swing. Music blared while immodest, drunken barang partied on the
decks. Some adventurous inebriated people whooped out loud and
then leaped on ropes, swinging past the rocks and dropping into the
river.

 Some of the more sensible life-jacketed tourists paddled sport
kayaks amid the chaos while wilder ones launched large inner tubes,
entered the rapid midstream current, then swept past Alan's group who
swerved to avoid being hit.

 A grateful Cambodian had started all this. He wanted to thank
the local aid workers by providing some fun while earning a few
dollars at the same time. At an accessible spot on the river, where a
paved road conveniently followed a curved valley into the jungle, he
had mounted a rope swing and found some inner tubes to ride the

strong current. Then he began selling drinks and food. It had soon morphed into a full-blown backpacker party scene.

Leng said, "Crazy barang." A loud scream from the swings caught everyone's attention. "Last month, three dead."

"Yeah, probably biology students," Alan said.

"No, two from Australia, one Swedish. But busy season is good." Leng waved at the chaos. "Not see us."

The three kayaks got past the party zone and soon evened up and traveled abreast once again.

"But six of us. Why so many?" Alan asked.

Sakda pointed at the three bowmen. "Hunt food, guard camp, build raft." He gestured toward Alan and Leng. "We get agarwood."

They paddled silently for a few minutes.

"Good kayaks. Thank you," Leng said.

Alan laughed. "Hiking into the Cardamom Range while avoiding land mines? Not for me, thanks. We'll go in style."

***

Betty occupied the far corner of a party hut deck. In her sweatpants and hoodie, she blended in with the party animals while she used her phone to discreetly take photos of Harry and Keat. Even though Keat was dressed in civilian clothes, the pair looked completely out of place, and the party people kept their distance and their voices muted. Harry was looking at the river through a pair of binoculars. Betty swung her focus to the river and saw the kayaks and paddlers get synced and pick up speed. They almost looked stylish. When the kayaks disappeared around the bend, Harry put down the binoculars and said to Keat, "You'd better keep track of them."

Keat took out his phone, tapped in a number, and issued some orders.

A young, paunchy, buttoned-down man ran out onto the deck. He went directly to Harry and said breathlessly, "Mr. Dunlap. Hello."

"What do you want?" Harry barked back at him.

"I'm here to meet you," he smiled and held out his card. "Hugh Humboldt ... from the embassy?"

Harry did not look pleased.

"I would have met you sooner, but ... uh, you didn't do the *in-country protocol* ... sir."

"I don't need a babysitter."

"Uh-huh. We learned of your presence here from our"— Humboldt glanced nervously at Keat—"Cambodian informants."

Harry laughed at this while Keat stayed poker-faced.

"Anyway, we just want to know how we can support you, sir."

Harry took the card and read it. "Okay, Humboldt, I'll be in touch." Harry walked away. Keat looked briefly adrift and then followed, leaving Humboldt alone and staring after them. From her corner, Betty got some good photos of Humboldt.

***

About an hour up the river, the expedition reached the trailhead of a large portage. The men struggled up the jungle trail with the kayaks and the packs. They sweated, swatted insects, and cursed. "It feels like we're climbing the Cardamom, after all," Alan said. They finally emerged into a clearing and put down their burdens. Looking over a cliff to the valley below, they saw that the jungle had been marred by a clear-cut scar beside the river. A bunch of abandoned trees were rotting in the mud. "Sophisticated agarwood harvest." Alan shook his head. "They got a permit for this?"

"Little bribe, big cut," Sakda said. "But more bad now. Go far in jungle." He pointed in the general direction they were headed. "Use helicopter. No need permit."

As if on cue, a helicopter came over the horizon and passed over them. They remained silent and pale for a few moments; no one wanted to voice their fears.

Alan shook off his ennui and looked around for the trail. "Okay, which way?"

Leng pointed out a small opening in the trees leading to a steep trail that went down into dense jungle. "Easy walk now … down the hill."

Alan nodded, then he and his kayak bowman, Kapono, picked up their kayak and started down the trail. Alan slipped on a muddy patch, then fell down on his back, pulling the kayak away from Kapono. The kayak slid on top of Alan, pinning him painfully.

He moaned, then recovered enough to tease Leng from under the kayak. "Easy walk."

Kapono lifted the kayak back up and off of Alan. Alan got up and started to brush off. Then Kapono slipped and let go. The kayak torpedoed into Alan and knocked him right over the cliff and out of sight. Everyone yelled; they rushed to the edge and peered over.

Alan hung upside down from a ledge fifteen feet below, hat still on by the chin strap, but his pants around his ankles, entwined on a stump. He looked up; everyone was too terrified to realize that he was out of immediate danger and looked ridiculous.

After a pause, Sakda laughed out loud, breaking the spell, and then the laugh caught on until even Alan joined in and said, "Really easy walk."

The men scrambled up top. They dropped a rope to Alan. He secured it around his hips, careful not to fall or drop his stuff. He turned, and a branch poked into his bare butt, popped his eyes wide open. He recovered and stood upright, got perched on the ledge, then pulled his pants up, regaining some dignity. He adjusted the sports cam on his vest, fingered his amulet, and gave them a thumbs-up. They pulled him toward the top.

Alan screamed out as he was attacked by a pit viper. They immediately slackened the rope, and Alan fell back and touched his neck. There was blood on his fingers. He recovered, steadied himself, and looked up at the snake wrapped around a tree above him. The pit viper hissed.

The hunters seemed to ignore him. They argued, then stopped. They had a plan!

Leng shouted, "Good luck!"

"Good luck?" Alan couldn't believe his ears.

"Yes, Kapono has his flute."

Alan rolled his eyes. Kapono removed a flute from his pack and played a hypnotic tune. Gradually the snake stopped hissing and wrapped itself back around the tree. Kapono gestured for silence as they pulled Alan up. When the snake snapped to attention, they stopped just in time.

"Got an electric guitar?" Alan asked. "Pit vipers, heavy metal fans." No one got the joke, of course. The hunters argued … *Boom!* A loud blast blew off the pit viper's head and ended the argument. The body uncoiled in slow motion and fell. Alan caught it, held it at arm's length, a little squeamish.

Sakda, holding a large shotgun, laughed again and praised Alan. "Good catch. Fresh meat!"

Alan looked at the snake, then shrugged and tied it to his belt. He warmly thanked Sakda. In a cooler voice, he said to Leng, "Just get me back up there."

They pulled Alan up to safety at the top of the cliff. Sakda moved in for a closer look at Alan's neck; Alan tried to wave him off.

"The snake bite? Oh, its nothing," he said, then collapsed. His body shook, trembled, and turned pale.

The men argued yet again. Sakda retrieved a pouch from his pack, took out a syringe, and filled it from a little bottle. Then he knelt beside Alan and gestured to Leng who ripped open Alan's shirt. Sakda plunged the syringe into Alan's chest.

After one of those brief moments that felt like eternity, Alan finally stopped trembling and seemed to sleep for a few minutes. He came to. Sakda propped him up against a rock and gave him a sip of water.

"Antivenom, strong medicine. You'll be okay," Leng said.

Sakda opened a vial of oil and rubbed some on Alan's neck. Alan inhaled, relaxed, and touched his amulet.

They eventually resumed their trek, descended the hill, and set up camp nearby the Teuk Vet Waterfall, whitewater rapids. This waterfall, and the grueling portage around it, kept most folks away from the jungle beyond. The hunters soon had a roaring fire going. They roasted the snake; everyone had a bite or two and watched the sunset.

Alan got up, a little pale and shaky. He followed Leng and Sakda out onto a point of land by the river. To the left, the river flowed fast toward them from around a bend. Below them, the river split, a ten-meter waterfall on one side and a gap leading to whitewater on the other. Leng pointed. "Kayak up river. Make camp. Then get Sakda's one tree."

Alan slumped, discouraged; the snakebite throbbed. Sakda noticed and tried to cheer him up. He pointed at the river. "Trip back, down river, very fast."

A clump of branches smashed against some rocks and broke up. Half of them plunged directly over the falls and disappeared, while the other half went through the gap and got churned up in the whitewater.

"In kayaks?" Alan turned paler.

"We build raft, carry the kayaks," Leng answered.

Alan laughed. "Okay! Something to look forward to."

***

The next day, they struggled against the current, passed high cliffs then muddy riversides with overhanging trees. The rain was constant, making the few rest stops uncomfortable.

Late in the evening they reached a fork in the river. Sakda led them into the other branch and then a short distance downstream, where he finally pointed at a riverside clearing with good access.

They stumbled ashore, made camp, then ate around a smoky fire and huddled under tarps. Sakda examined Alan's snakebite and applied some agarwood oil. Alan inhaled and relaxed.

More Fieldwork

The perpetual Phnom Penh traffic jam crept through the streets at sunset. Keat's SUV waited in traffic with a bunch of motorbikes trapped behind. The riders were all anonymous, faces hidden by helmets and dust masks. At this time of year the rain forest in the Cardamom was still wet, but Phnom Penh was hot and dry. The SUV lurched forward, creating a tiny gap, and the bikes all squeezed past. A tall, slim rider on a big motorcycle slowed, pulled off to the side, and waited in front of a parked truck. The SUV passed, and the rider followed at a distance.

The SUV pulled up to the Vattanac Tower. Keat and Harry got out, gave the keys to a valet, and went inside. The motorcycle went past and was parked discreetly out on the street; the rider dismounted, and the helmet came off—it was Betty, in baggy clothing with her hair in a ponytail.

Betty would not accept the role of victim. She was an agent, a proactive fighter who did not like to witness or experience abuse. So while the *boys* were off in the jungle—and they hadn't even *thought* of apologizing for not inviting her!—she investigated the "bad guys," as she called them. Getting past their ineffective firewalls online, she'd scooped up lots of information in a few short hours, then happily headed for Phnom Penh and gone stalking in person.

Betty stretched, donned a baseball cap, and walked into the tower, head down. She went directly to the Salvatore Ferragamo fashion boutique, where the outfits cost more than what most Cambodians earned in a year. Fortunately, Betty was well-armed with credit cards. She found some lovely but demure clothing to wear as urban camouflage.

Betty emerged from the boutique dressed like a rich tourist, her baggy clothes well-hidden in a Ferragamo shopping bag. She took the elevator to the thirty-seventh floor Rosewood Hotel lobby and donned a large pair of sunglasses. On the Sora Bar deck, she found a discreet spot and ordered coffee. To support her role as a tourist, she began taking photos of the Phnom Penh views.

A few tables away, Harry and Keat Chhon were sitting with a beautiful Asian lady. Though Betty didn't recognize her, she was immediately suspicious: guilty by association. Then she suppressed a more primitive emotion, a little envy.

Betty watched and caught some of the conversation. Harry was persuasive, then aggressive, but he appeared to fail to convince this skeptical, articulate woman of whatever he was proposing. Betty started to upwardly revise her opinion of the mysterious belle and managed to sneak several photos of them while snapping her scenery pictures.

Bungle in the Jungle

The hunters woke to an overcast sky in the damp, gloomy dawn, stiff from the kayaks. Sakda examined Alan's swollen neck under his unshaven chin and applied more oil, then gave Kapono instructions on raft building.

A sudden loud noise startled them; a helicopter appeared out of the heavy clouds. They got a brief glimpse before it disappeared back into the clouds. "Were those logs? Hanging from the copter?" Alan asked.

"Yes," Leng and Sakda said at the same time.

They gaped at the clouds. The helicopter poachers had obviously found and harvested a valuable tree. And they appeared to be coming from the area that Sakda had pointed out as their destination.

Sakda grabbed his pack and set off into the jungle. Alan and Leng checked their gear, hefted their packs, and ran to catch up.

Sakda and Leng hiked up a steep trail. Alan tried to keep up, but he slipped, fell, and panicked when a large spider dropped on his arm. He brushed it off, and then another spider landed. He snapped this one off, looked up, and saw a mass of spiders above. He blanched, but adrenaline soon kicked in. He got to his feet and scrambled up the trail.

He caught up to the others, then stumbled. Leng steadied him and spoke with Sakda. He removed one of Alan's packs and handed it to Sakda, who secured it to Leng's load.

"Treasure, next valley. Not far," Sakda said.

They continued their gloomy trek, gloomier still when it started to rain.

Sakda recognized a landmark. He'd found the little opening he'd been looking for. He smiled for the first time in a long while and plunged through the greenery. Leng and Alan rushed to stay close behind him, then almost knocked him over. Sakda stared incredulously at a small clear-cut; freshly felled trees were lying all around.

"They take. Take one tree."

The helicopter poachers had done their ugly work. Without the skills to identify the individual trees as agarwood, they'd simply cut everything in sight, taken whatever agarwood they could find, and abandoned the rest. Catastrophe!

The three men trudged back into the camp at dusk and something smelled delicious; some small mammals roasting on a spit. Their pace quickened, and Alan's spirits lifted a bit ... until they shared the bad news.

After eating, they argued about what to do next. They had prepared for a quick operation, just a couple of days in the jungle; they hadn't planned on an extended stay. It seemed like there were lots of good reasons to abandon their quest.

"Find new treasure." Sakda was insistent. "Sakda can find."

Alan could relate to that. The others eventually came around to the same view. The camp crew would spend less time building the raft and more time hunting and gathering. There was an abundance of food in the jungle, if you knew where to look. And how to catch it or harvest it.

***

Back in the rainy jungle the next day, Alan, Leng, and Sakda were paused on a trail. Alan was again having trouble keeping pace, and Sakda was concerned. Leng came to Alan's aid by repacking yet again. His load got bigger while Alan's shrank to a single backpack.

Sakda looked closely at Alan's neck and pale face under his new beard. He didn't like what he saw. "Back to camp."

But Alan pushed him away. "No. I'm okay." He looked at Leng, who was now carrying most of his stuff and said, "Thanks." He started up the trail, determined, but before they could follow, he tripped on a branch.

Although it wasn't a branch, but rather a startled snake that slithered away. Alan got up. A dark figure swung down from the trees and landed right in front of him; Alan stared straight into the eyes of a fierce jungle warrior.

Alan looked to Leng and Sakda for rescue. Another warrior appeared, grabbed Leng. A third warrior came for Sakda. Sakda moved faster than his assailant was expecting and held him at bay; they eyeballed each other, stony faced.

"Phnheaphaael!" Sakda said, then he laughed. The warrior laughed back, and the mood changed.

The other two warriors released Alan and Leng, joined their companion, and talked to Sakda in the Khmer Loeu hill tribe language. Lots of gestures and laughs.

After a few minutes, Sakda pointed to Alan then touched his own neck. The Khmer Loeu warriors took a close look at Alan; he flinched under the close attention of these fierce men. The three warriors nodded, spoke to Sakda, and then disappeared into the jungle.

Without another word, Sakda walked away and up the path. Leng and Alan exchanged a "what's up?" look and caught up to Sakda.

"Khmer Loeu?" Leng asked.

Sakda nodded.

"They live here?" Alan said. "Should we leave?" Leng said at the same time.

"No worry," Sakda replied and walked on without further explanation. Alan saw that Leng shared his frustration. They shrugged and followed Sakda farther into the jungle.

They stopped here and there to cut branches down. Sure enough, most of these branches had some agarwood inside, and Alan learned how to identify infected trees. On their return trek, they dragged the agarwood branches back to camp. If they didn't find a big treasure, at least they'd return with something from the jungle.

At dusk, Alan slumped into the campsite behind Leng and Sakda. It was busy with activity despite the relentless rain. Under a tarp, Kapono cooked dinner at a smoky fire while the other men worked by the river.

***

The next morning, the rain let up. Sakda inspected the raft work—they'd found enough food—and gave some advice.

He grabbed his pack then beckoned Leng and Alan to follow him into the jungle. Leng helped Alan, who struggled to keep up. They soon met up with the Khmer Loeu warriors again, this time without the dramatic mock ambush.

The warriors talked with Sakda and stared at Alan, who squirmed under the attention. Sakda accepted something and held it out to Alan. "Eat," he said.

Alan blanched at the sight of the gooey leaf and turned away.

"Khmer Loeu snake medicine. Gift from Chief Rithy. Good. You eat."

Alan took the leaf, looked closer at it, grimaced, then stuffed it in his mouth and tried to swallow. Leng shoved a water bottle at him, and he managed to wash the vile concoction down his throat. He shuddered, then finally recovered with a twisted grin.

Sakda thanked the warriors; Alan hesitated, finally adding his thanks and getting a brief nod in acknowledgment. Sakda bid farewell, and the Khmer Loeu faded back into the jungle. The three agarwood hunters resumed their trek.

Here Comes the Sun

Alone and exhausted two days later, Alan scrambled up a hill and stumbled on a root as he reached the top. He tried to stand up but fell back down. Sitting on the jungle floor, sweat stung his eyes and blurred his vision. He swatted at a mosquito next to his snakebite. The crude Khmer Loeu medicine fought it out with the last of the snake venom in his system. Alan, overcome by the jungle's heat, noises, and shadows, panicked and called out, "Leng! Sakda!"

He got no answer from the dark forest; he gave up. He took his Iridium satellite phone from his small pack, pulled the antenna out, found his GPS coordinates and began to input a text message:

- airlift needed URGENT.

Then he checked his latitude and entered 12.215N.

Alan paused. He touched his amulet and thought about Nazneen languishing far away. He shook his head, looked at his phone, and frowned. He canceled the text message, put the phone away, picked up his pack, turned on his sports cam, and headed up the hill.

He caught up just in time to see Leng and Sakda disappear around a corner in the trail; then he heard a whoop of joy. He hurried up the trail, turned the corner, and joined his companions in the open air of a large forest clearing.

Alan beheld a large, round, natural pool, fed by a waterfall cascading over a cliff above the clearing. The sun broke out of the clouds for the first time in days, and diamonds glittered on the pool.

Sakda grinned. He looked pleased to have found this spot again; he looked around, always vigilant, always checking for danger. Satisfied, he dropped his pack and stripped off his clothes, then hid his things under a rock and dove into the pool. Leng laughed at Alan and then stripped, hid his own stuff, and joined Sakda in the pool.

Alan touched his neck and found the swelling almost gone. He got naked, hid his stuff, and dove into the cool water. The three men frolicked like young boys and found a loose vine to use as a swing. They took turns swinging out and dive bombing each other with big splashes. Finally they stretched out on the rocks in the sun and marveled about their respite from the gloomy trek.

After they shared some food and water, Sakda watched Alan learn how to fight. Leng showed how a small man could overcome a bigger opponent. Alan caught on and even got the better of Leng in the final bout.

The lesson was done; Alan dove into the pool and floated on his back. He drifted into a sunny spot … *paradise.*

A sudden noise cut his reverie short. It got louder.

Sakda grabbed the water bottle, gestured urgently, then dove in and swam under the waterfall. Alan and Leng followed closely and held their breath underwater. When Alan came up for air, he saw Harry in the helicopter door, and sank back down under the water. He waited until he was out of breath then carefully surfaced again. He saw the copter rise and fly away down the river.

The three men came out from under the falls. Alan's grim mood was echoed on his companions' faces. They silently got dressed and resumed their hunt.

***

By the next day Alan felt better, moved more fluidly, and the swelling was completely gone from his neck. He emerged from the dense jungle and onto a cliff top crowned by several large trees. At the bottom of the cliff, far below them, the river snaked through the canyon. Leng and Sakda sat together on the cliff edge. They were looking back along the side of the canyon to the recent clear-cut where the poachers had beaten them to the one tree. The rains were already washing away the exposed ground. Alan was going to join them but gulped and stayed back a bit; it was a long way down.

Leng was looking discouraged, and even Sakda's stoic gaze showed hints of despair. Alan's good mood vanished—their quest had failed. They sat silent for a few minutes staring at the clear-cut.

The sun emerged from behind a dark cloud. Sakda swallowed and peered intensely just below the clear-cut. The bright light had revealed something that had caught his keen eye. Muttering to himself, he jumped up, grabbed his pack, and ran back into the bush. Leng and Alan exchanged puzzled glances, then ran after him.

They raced through the forest to the clear-cut and found Sakda climbing down to a ledge some feet below. A ledge that was newly exposed. The heavy rain had washed away mud and debris from the clear-cut above, changed the direction of the runoff, and cleared this ledge. Sakda clawed and pulled away rotting wood, then leaned in to sniff.

"Khmer khlem," (Cambodian agarwood), Sakda said and smiled. Alan and Leng climbed down to join him, and they soon uncovered the remains of a large tree, parts of which where rotted and fell apart at their touch. Large pieces of agarwood remained. A fortuitous windfall that satisfied both meanings of the word. Nature and time had done all the work of extracting the treasure. They simply had to pack it up and carry it back to camp. They'd hit the jackpot!

Alan took in the amazing scent; it tantalized every atom in his being. He and Leng grinned and high-fived each other, then Alan turned on his cam. Sakda and Leng got their ropes and axes out and went to work. Alan joined them, and they soon formed an efficient team. They pulled the pieces back up to the clear-cut and bundled them together.

Sakda looked back and forth at the bundles, nodded to himself, and smiled. He looked up and said, "More agarwood, more than one tree."

They grinned widely—this treasure was worth much more than the tree they'd lost, perhaps even more than what they needed. They hid some of the bundles and headed back with the others; it would take two trips and more help to get this back to camp. Hard but joyful work lay ahead of them.

***

They got all the treasure back to camp in good weather, then took a break to enjoy the sunshine and breeze. Alan, completely healed and coached by Leng, sparred with Kapono. He toppled his much bigger opponent and battled him to a tie. They laughed then disengaged and dusted themselves off. Break over, the raft construction resumed in earnest.

Alan went to do some digital chores. He switched the batteries in his solar panel charger, then copied all the video he had captured onto his phone. He set up an app that would back up the phone to the cloud as soon as it found a data signal. Then he relaxed and watched the others working on the raft. They'd built a base of big logs and were splitting some smaller logs to make rough, thick boards. The boards would create a deck for the raft, hold it together, and make it easier for the men to move around on top and navigate. He had a brainstorm and called Sakda over. As he pointed to various parts of the raft and explained his idea, Sakda started laughing. Alan faltered; he noticed that Leng looked miffed. Sakda also noticed and stopped laughing.

"Leng. Come," Sakda shouted.

"Bring the others," Alan said.

Getting Out

Harry perched in the open helicopter door, searching the river below for signs of Alan's group. So far, nothing, another fruitless day. And what for? Helping a private company secure the field for their new drug. Following orders that came directly from the White House. Both unprecedented in his long career. The media sold the story that the denizens of the "deep state," people like Harry, were secretly in control of their government. Nope. They'd all ceded their sovereignty to a far more sinister group: corporations.

The copter flew over a fork in the river; a kayak emerged from the forest canopy at the river's edge. Harry saw two men in the kayak—one with white hair—and signaled to Keat in the copilot's seat. The copter descended and followed the kayak down the river.

***

Their beards were a little thicker, and the camp was packed up. After ten days of hard work—first paddling upstream, then searching the jungle, finding the treasure, and building the raft—it was time to go home.

The chatty, happy team loaded equipment, two of the kayaks, a pile of agarwood branches, and a few of the precious pieces onto the raft. Alan checked that his amulet was on his neck, fixed his sports cam to his life jacket, then attached another one at the front of the raft looking back. He double-checked his phone/cloud storage setup, then he linked the cams to the phone so they'd upload live video once online.

A buzzing sound in the distance alerted them to a searching helicopter. Sakda and his bowman boarded the third kayak, then paddled out from under the trees and into the current where they picked up some speed and headed downriver.

Back on shore, they got a glimpse of Harry in the open door before the copter changed direction to follow Sakda. They stayed still, well hidden under some trees. Soon, both Sakda and the helicopter were out of sight and sound.

The rest of the team boarded the raft, set off in the opposite direction. They poled, slow and hard, upriver and against the current, until they got back to where the river forked. They poled even harder and finally got around the bend and into the branch of the river they'd paddled up ten days before. They caught the current and headed downriver.

They retraced their route into the Cardamom, making their way downriver in a fraction of the time it had taken to go against the current. The rain that had afflicted their hunt had also soaked the watershed, topped up the river, and made the current even faster.

PING. Alan heard his phone find the Xanadu wireless data signal and smiled; the auto-backup was underway. He started video capture on his cam. As planned, the live video streamed directly through his phone to the cloud.

The overhanging trees on the shorelines gave way to steeper rocky riverbanks; the river narrowed, and the raft picked up speed. It tilted to one side in the strong current, but the team held on tight. They went faster.

"Keep right," Leng screamed at Alan who steered hard and gripped the rudder, barely missing the big rocks while hitting the smaller ones.

Keep right, keep right. Alan pushed the tiller. They crashed on a rock and rolled; the kayaks got loose and flew off the raft. Alan avoided the biggest rock then looked dead ahead and saw the kayaks disappear over the Teuk Vet Waterfalls. "Holy crap."

"The gap," Leng shouted, pointing to the right, then he resumed paddling.

The men paddled, and Alan pushed the tiller until they just

managed to squeeze through the gap. They dropped, again and again, but somehow the raft held together and the men hung on.

They found themselves becalmed on a slower side channel surrounded by trees. They relaxed and cheered … but then the raft went around a bend, and the cheers dropped off.

Two cops in bush gear waited for them on their pontoon boat downriver. The current took the raft right to this spot. Alan recognized Samphy, but he didn't know the skinny cop. Leng whispered, "They kill us." Alan's hand went immediately to his amulet; he frowned, shook his head, and his lips formed a silent no.

"Hands up, poachers," Samphy yelled. "Kosal!" He got his partner's attention and pointed. Kosal snagged the raft with a grappling hook and pulled it to their boat. Samphy boarded the raft to Leng's protests. Samphy pistol-whipped Leng. He went down, and Samphy kicked him hard in the gut.

"Hey," Alan shouted and grabbed Samphy's arm. He saved Leng from the hardest blow yet, but Samphy immediately swung the gun around and hit Alan on the forehead. Now he had bloodied both of them.

"Enough!" Kosal yelled out. He gestured. "Everyone off."

Leng staggered from his wound as Samphy herded them off the raft. Alan leaned down to help him.

"Yes, they'll kill us," Leng said.

"Police." Alan spit the word out like it was poison.

Samphy pulled them apart and forced them to kneel with the others. Leng changed tactics. "Take it all."

"Thanks, we will." Samphy laughed.

Kosal yelled out in Khmer. He motioned for Samphy to step back and aimed his gun at the team kneeling on the shore. He picked Alan as a priority target and cocked his rifle.

Thwunk! Kosal got an arrow through his forehead and it seemed like slow motion as he dropped into the water. Khmer Loeu warriors swarmed out of the trees.

Samphy jumped onto the boat, fired up the engine, and sped away. His partner bled the muddy water red.

The warriors whooped. A tall, proud warrior stepped out of the trees carrying a rifle and a bow, carefully aimed his rifle, and fired a shot at Samphy. He missed his now distant target, but did hit a pontoon. The pontoon deflated; the boat listed sideways and slowed as it went around a bend.

The warriors cleared a path for their handsome chief—so young, yet so full of gravitas. He strolled to the raft, examined it, and surveyed the team of four. He paid extra attention to Alan and his snakebite, then spoke to his warriors. Leng listened closely to the chief and tried out his Khmer Loeu dialect. After three attempts to communicate, the chief laughed and said, "Good lucky day for you!"

Alan and Leng laughed along with the chief who then introduced himself, patting his chest. "Rithy," he said.

Alan patted his own chest. "Alan," he said and then looked at Leng who followed suit. Rithy smiled and gave them a little courtesy bow.

Two more warriors showed up from downriver in the missing kayaks and spoke with Rithy, who grinned and relayed their message. "Boat go down, bad cop run to forest."

Meanwhile, Alan recognized the three men who'd provided his snakebite medicine. They were stripping Kosal, the dead cop. Alan gestured at the body. "Jungle justice, huh?"

Rithy liked the alliteration, tried out the words, "Jun-gle Justice. Yeah!"

"But many thanks to you … and your men."

"Yes, many thanks." Rithy bowed. "But now, you must pay the

Khmer Loeu."

The warriors picked up the naked corpse and asked their chief a question. He answered, and they carried the body away into the jungle. Rithy grinned at Alan. "The Warmbu will eat good this night."

Alan looked squeamishly to Leng for a translation, but Leng just shrugged.

Rithy pointed to the kayaks. "Boats, we keep. And all this." He pointed to the equipment and the agarwood on the raft. "We keep. You keep log boat." He saw Alan and Leng exchange troubled looks and said, "Maran downriver, not far."

"Don't have much choice," Alan said softly.

"Lucky we're alive," Leng said.

Rithy gave orders to his warriors. They took the equipment, the agarwood, and the kayaks into the jungle. Leng and the other two boarded the raft.

Rithy himself removed the solar panel and sports cam attached to Alan's life jacket; Alan reminded himself that all the video, including the recent ambush, had been auto-uploaded to the cloud via the Xanadu data access. Rithy handled Alan's smart phone and frowned. Finally, he found and admired Alan's satellite phone.

"Let us keep our smart phones," Alan said and pointed at his. "They work around here okay, but in most of the jungle they don't work. No signal." He pointed at the satellite phone. "That one will be useful; it works almost everywhere. I'll give you the password and show you how to use it."

Rithy nodded, so Alan gave him instructions for the satellite phone. That done, he turned to the river.

Rithy shouted at him to wait, then picked a smaller piece from the pile of confiscated agarwood. He looked strangely at Alan, said something in his tribal tongue, and gave him the piece. Alan was baffled. Rithy smiled and said, "Yes. Moon Quest. When you be ready."

Alan looked again to Leng for an explanation and got another "I don't know" shrug.

Alan joined the others on the raft, and they pushed off and floated downriver in the fading daylight. They looked a little glum, watching the happy warriors disappear into the jungle.

***

Alan, Leng, and crew brought the conspicuously empty raft to the Maran riverside, where Sakda and Betty chatted in the dark night. She saw them first, shone a flashlight at them, and said, "Traveling light?" She and Sakda laughed out loud.

"Glad someone's amused," Alan said. "I don't like playing cops and robbers ... especially when the cops are robbers."

"Sorry." Sakda sobered up. "Khmer Loeu slow, come late."

"The Khmer Loeu came late?" Alan couldn't believe his ears. "You ... hold on!"

Sakda waved off the discussion and barked an order at the three Cambodians on the raft. They chopped at the ropes that bound the raft together.

"The Khmer Loeu got your agarwood?" Betty said. "That sucks."

Alan, Leng, and Sakda exchanged a mischievous look and couldn't suppress their grins.

"Not all of it," Alan said.

They pulled up one of the rough boards that decked the raft. Alan reached into a cavity in the uncovered log and pulled out a dark piece of agarwood. "We hid it. Inside the raft."

"We saved the best stuff," Leng said. "Idea from Alan."

"He think good," Sakda said. "For barang."

"Okay, it trumps steganography!" Betty said with a big smile.

They dismantled the raft and collected the dark wood pieces, then took a break at the riverbank. Betty listened to the story of the jungle hunt, the raft ride, and the narrow escape from the bad cops. All the while, they kept fawning over their glorious stash.

Eventually Alan turned to Sakda and asked, "What is a Moon Quest?"

Sakda nodded. "Before. Maran have medicine man. Sakda do Moon Quest."

"What is it?"

"Eat medicine, visit other place…"

"And?" Alan wanted to know more.

Sakda nodded again and was about to answer.

"Biggest treasure, ever," Leng interrupted and pointed back at the logs.

"Big risk," Sakda said.

"Get it up the hill," Alan said. "The sooner it's refined and stored in oil barrels, the better."

"Much danger," Sakda said.

"Maybe we should wait? Till things cool down?" Betty said.

"No! We can't wait," Alan said. "Besides, it's about time to send our regular shipment through Phnom Penh. I'll go get the truck to move the treasure."

Breakthrough Break-in Blowup

They moved the precious cargo up to the plantation under the cover of darkness—the fewer people who knew about it, the better—and finished just as the old truck broke down. After a shave, a long shower, and a bit of sleep, Alan went to the cookhouse, grabbed some food from Tevy, and headed for the lab.

Leng fed a fire under a large outdoor still. Alan rubbed his freshly shaved chin. The university research called for agarwood distillation at a high temperature, hotter than the traditional process.

"Hot enough?" Alan asked.

"Plenty hot."

"Temp?"

"Over two hundred," Leng said. Alan stared back, and Leng raised his voice a notch. "We use your new plan, no worry."

"Okay, bring me the first two liters for the assay lab work, and barrel the rest for shipment." He went to the lab and worked at his screen.

Betty wandered in from the lab annex, puzzled by her phone. "I did some snooping while you played Boy Scout in the jungle. Look at these." She showed Alan some photos. "Who is the femme fatale with Harry and Keat?"

Alan was shocked dumb by the Sora Bar photos—Yuying meeting with Harry and Keat. He fiddled with the bio-catalyzer to mask his reaction. And he'd really liked Yuying, despite her questionable overture. Glancing out the window, he saw Leng processing their own contraband. *Who am I to judge?*

Sakda strode into the lab holding up a freshly cut piece of wood with a dark agarwood stain. "Sakda find good agarwood. In G."

"In the G section?" Alan came alert. "We tried a new infection protocol there. But only last year. It was supposed to take two more years before we'd see significant resin production in the trees."

"He means it's too soon," Betty said to Sakda.

Sakda rubbed at the heartwood then sniffed his oily fingers. "Strong!"

Alan stared at the piece. *If Sakda is impressed, it must be superb.*

Sakda held his fingers up to Alan's nose. Alan reacted to the scent then took the piece and examined it. Sakda said, "Like best agarwood, from jungle."

"You're right! It's incredible!" Alan said. *Did we just solve the grow problems?* He looked at Sakda. "If we can replicate this success we'll have our breakthrough."

"He wants you to check around. See if there is more of this," Betty said.

"Yes, please. Check out all of G. Look at the K section too." They'd applied the new method in K, right after doing G.

***

Three days later, Alan had a new beard, and his hair was askew. He'd worked almost around the clock, had taken power naps waiting for lab results. Betty was busy in the annex with her headphones on. The pen on Alan's plotter stopped; Alan jumped up, pulled the paper out, and taped it over a similar page already on the window. The graph lines from the two pages matched up. Alan smiled.

Betty noticed Alan's activity, tugged off her headphones, and joined him at the window to admire his handiwork. "You know we can do a digital overlay? There's no need for paper."

"I like paper," Alan said, engrossed in his output. Then he snapped to attention. "This is it!"

"You sure?"

"The assay is a close match. Repeatable results … from separate runs." He laughed. "It would even pass peer review." *If all my peers haven't been bought off.*

"Fantabulous!"

Alan pointed to Sakda's samples from G and K, all premium quality agarwood. "And I think we may have solved the grow problems. Paired with the new distilling protocol, it would mean that anyone could produce the high-grade oil."

"Congrats, Alan. You've done it."

Alan paused. "We've done it." He grinned at Betty, for once escaping his egocentrism.

Betty laughed, and glowed, obviously delighted by the praise.

"This data is ready for prime time," Alan said.

"Great, I'll publish it."

Alan envisioned Nazneen at a porn website. "Not yet. I need to be ready. We've only got one chance to get past SpringenRx and their spin doctors. But first"—even though it delayed publishing their research—"Batar needs the treasure; they can't wait."

"Huh? Kapono and Sakda took it yesterday, with the regular shipment."

They'd somehow revived the old plantation truck.

"And Leng and I are going to meet them in Phnom Penh."

"You'll be an outlaw."

Alan stared, then shrugged. "Input and integrate the new data," he said, then remembered his manners. "Please."

He took the OPAL key fob from his pocket, plugged it in, and put his thumb on it. The PC chimed, and the screen refreshed with a green text—"Access Granted." "Here you go," he said, then stopped and turned very serious. "Keep it safe."

"Data management…" She grabbed the laptop, held it proprietorially, and gave Alan a fierce look. "My department."

Chastened, Alan shrugged. "Okay, I'm going to bed, got an early start tomorrow."

***

Loud ska music played inside Betty's big headphones. She swayed right along to her personal soundtrack, working alone in the lab annex in the dead of night. She'd created yet another new outfit by deftly recombining elements of those previously worn. She worked at her computer, enjoying the splendid isolation; even the door to the main lab was shut tight. *I'm just so productive when all the distractions are … asleep.* Using local Wi-Fi to connect with the OPAL-enabled laptop in the main lab, she sent the new data to safe, encrypted sites in the cloud.

***

In the dark hour before dawn, and just before his alarm sounded, Alan woke up and sniffed the air. He walked through the quiet plantation to the cookhouse, where he found Tevy already making breakfast. Grabbing a bowl of chicken-boiled rice, he headed for the lab and entered through the main door.

Wham! He got pushed forward and landed smack down, face on the floor, covered in warm, wet rice. Harry loomed above him in the doorway and pointed a gun. Alan groaned. "What the f—?"

"Shut yer trap." Harry hit him then pulled him up, farther into the lab, and tied him to a post. Blood dripped from the reopened wound in his forehead and got in his eyes. Harry searched the lab, then sat down at the laptop on Alan's desk.

Harry clicked the mouse, punched keys, then read the screen. "What have we here?" Harry leaned over the side, found the OPAL fob in the USB port, pulled it out, and chuckled. "Could this be the key to your heart?" Harry pocketed the fob. "Or to something more important?" He smashed up the laptop, went over to the bio-catalyzer and fiddled with the controls. "The bio-catalyzer, so sensitive." Still chuckling, he detached a tube then reattached it to another socket.

"That's pure butane!" shouted Alan.

"The great scientist. Such a waste."

"You haven't thought this through … the consequences—"

"You think anyone cares what happens in this godforsaken backwater?" Harry pulled a lever on the main pipe. The machine beeped, and its little screen flashed a yellow warning message. "Have a blast, buddy," he said as he ran out of the lab.

Alan struggled with the ropes and tested the strength of the post. The machine beeped faster. He screamed, "Help, help! In the lab. Help!"

***

Behind the thick annex door, Betty thought she heard something. She took off her headphones and listened carefully. Complete silence. She shrugged, put the phones back on, and resumed her work, bopping along again to her music.

***

Alan gave up, slumped down the pole, and his phone fell out of his pocket. He stared at it for a bit then blinked. *Who ya gonna call?* He contorted himself to reach the phone, tapped on it with one finger. The bio-catalyzer screen blinked red, warning *OVERLOAD*. Alan managed to select an address, one of his group contacts, The A-Team. He then tapped out HLP LAB NOW and hit Send.

***

On Betty's screen, an instant message window popped up with a text from Alan:

- HLP LAB NOW.

Briefly baffled, Betty tore off her headphones, ran to the door, and slid it open. "What's happ—?"

"Quick, untie me; it's going to blow."

The bio-catalyzer whistled, leaked vapor, and shook. Betty calmly fiddled with the controls.

Alan pushed himself up. "What are you doing?"

Betty flipped a switch up. The machine vibrated even harder. She flinched, flipped it down, and the vibration and vapor stream slowed down. Alan sighed in relief. Betty walked over and pulled at the main lever. The vapor stopped, and she untied Alan.

"Whew! Thanks, but next time—"

"Boys are so impatient."

"You have balls!"

Leng rushed in. "You need help?"

"Not anym—actually, yeah. Harry paid us a visit." Alan waved at the mess. "He took the OPAL. We've got to get it back."

"We can catch Harry."

Alan agreed with a curt nod and started toward the door. Then he stopped, turned back, toyed with his amulet, and pointed at the aborted bio-catalyzer bomb. "Maybe not …" Alan said, sounding strangely wistful. "Maybe it'd be better if I died." He turned back, headed for the door.

Betty looked at Leng, but he just shrugged; they followed Alan out the door.

***

Harry came down the road, out of the forest, and walked across the Maran bridge toward the SUV where Keat Chhon waited. Harry pointed back up the hill and grinned triumphantly at Keat. Before Keat could say anything, Harry's phone rang. "Yeah?"

"I need that key fob," Humboldt said from the other end.

"Got it. Know what's better? I got rid of Grace along with all his work."

"Radical! The coup de grâce, huh?"

"Nope, blew him up," Harry said, looking back up the hill.

A huge cloud of debris appeared above the trees at the top of the hill, followed immediately by a loud boom. Harry heard a faint curse from the phone; Humboldt must have pulled the phone away from his ear. Then the voice got louder. "You, you blew—"

"I'll send the fob. Figure it out, and get me access to the data. Gotta go." He ended the call and looked at Keat. "Let's go have a look for … *salvage*." Harry grinned, very pleased with himself.

They drove up the hill as dawn was breaking. Harry hid in the trees outside the plantation gate and looked through his binoculars. He saw a real but harmless mess of debris about fifty meters away from the lab, then blinked hard as the sun breached the horizon and blazed his binocular-enhanced sight. He went right back to the SUV, got in, and scowled at Keat before they drove away.

***

Alan, Betty, Kapono, and Leng surveyed the aftermath of the staged explosion in the brightening dawn light. Alan relaxed a little. "Might keep them guessing for a while, buy us some time."

Leng stayed behind with Kapono and packed up the detonator while Alan went to the lab with Betty. She danced along beside him and said, "That rocked. So authentic. Playground of Chaos will never be the same."

Just as the sun came up, Alan glanced back and saw a small flash, off in the distance, just outside the plantation gate. He looked hard but saw nothing more and went into the lab with Betty. They surveyed the mess Harry had left behind. Alan was grim. "I need my data."

"I'll take care of Harry and get the fob back. You make sure the treasure gets safely to Batar."

Alan was quiet for a minute, but Betty's confidence was infectious, and he rallied.

"Okay."

Losing It

Two guards stood by the gates of a barbed wire-enclosed security compound under a sign: Phnom Penh Export Clearance. Two more guards stood inside the yard by the customs building—a shed with an air conditioner. Leng and Alan sheltered in the shed's shade near where they'd parked. They watched their ancient plantation truck enter the yard and pull into the shade. Kapono exited the driver's door. Sakda emerged from the passenger side and laughed out loud.

"You made it!" Alan laughed along and gave them both a hug.

An inspector in a trim uniform came out of the shed and looked in the back of the truck. Leng gave him the first of three export permits. He read the document while they unloaded the barrels and bags and sorted it onto skids. The inspector then compared the goods to the paperwork. Looking at Alan, he gestured toward the skids. "All from one place? Grace Agarwood?"

"Yes sir," Alan said.

The inspector peered at the barrels, then consulted the paperwork again; Alan tried to relax. It didn't help that Leng was trying hard not to look nervous, so Alan moved in closer to Sakda who was typically aloof. He noticed that one of the guards, the really nasty-looking one, was watching, and he shifted again to block the guard's view.

"No good," the inspector said.

Yikes.

Leng said, "This very good—"

"No stamp. No department stamp."

Alan suppressed a sigh of relief. "Look on the last page."

Leng relaxed; Sakda waited patiently.

The inspector flipped to the last page and looked a little

disappointed. He gestured impatiently to Leng for the other two permits. Alan intercepted them, slipped a hundred-dollar bill into each, then handed them over. Now the inspector was very happy.

Outside the yard, a fancy white limo approached the gates. It stopped; the driver spoke with the guards and was waved through. Two Bataris got out of the limo, formally greeted Alan and the inspector, and briefly acknowledged the others.

The whole group gathered round the skids, checking the papers, discussing the goods. The inspector took renewed interest in two of the barrels, double-checking them against the paperwork. Alan's jitters resumed.

One of the Bataris went back to the limo and fetched a stunning Thai beauty whom he introduced to the inspector. The inspector lost all interest in the skids—he shamelessly flirted as they disappeared into the customs shed.

Alan smiled, paused, then directed the Bataris to focus on the same two barrels that had caught the inspector's interest. He lowered his voice. "Take special care with these." The Bataris nodded.

When Alan noticed that the nasty guard was still listening and now seemed to be taking photos with his phone, he put his arm around Leng in another blocking maneuver, then they loaded the goods back into the truck. Kapono got behind the wheel and Leng got in the passenger seat while Alan and Sakda got in the Land Cruiser and the Bataris got in their limo.

Just the four guards, and the empty skids remained in the yard. Alan looked closer at the nasty guard who was again very busy with his phone. *Definitely Harry's kind of guy.* Then he glanced at the customs shed and became concerned for the safety of the young Thai. *What if...?* As the small convoy left the yard, Alan called the Bataris and was reassured that they'd researched the inspector enough to know that their distraction-cum-bribe would be fine—in fact, more than safe.

As the small convoy crept through traffic, the limo fell behind the other two vehicles. Alan and Sakda came to an abrupt halt, directly behind the freight truck, trapped between some of the dilapidated French colonial buildings of Phnom Penh and the endless construction sites that were rapidly obliterating them. The stalled traffic was squeezed into a single lane by street vendors, construction mess, and busy crowds; meanwhile, the motorbikes and tuk-tuks somehow kept moving, darting in, out, and around all obstacles. The freight truck moved forward a bit, leaving a small gap between it and Alan's Land Cruiser. A street vendor pushed a cart into the gap then ran away.

As the traffic jam cleared up, the freight truck moved forward about ten meters, and Alan realized that his vehicle was effectively trapped. Leng and Kapono stuck their heads out of the truck and looked back at them with puzzled faces.

Harry and Samphy dashed out from the crowd. Sakda and Alan scrambled out of the Land Cruiser, yelled out a warning, and struggled past the cart, but they were too late to prevent an attack.

Harry pulled Leng down to the street and pistol-whipped him while Samphy boarded the truck on the driver's side and subdued Kapono. Harry jumped into the passenger seat. The truck took off just as Alan tried to jump on the back. He missed his footing and fell off. He sprang back up, dusted himself off, then he and Sakda helped Leng to his feet. The truck barreled away.

By the time they pushed the abandoned cart out of the way, the road was again jammed up with traffic, and they were still stuck. Alan hailed a tuk-tuk; the three men squeezed in, and Alan shoved a handful of bills at the driver and pointed at the distant truck. The tuk-tuk driver, drunk on the wad of cash, took every risk he could. They drove up on the sidewalk, almost hit pedestrians, then wove in and out of oncoming traffic, barely avoiding head-on collisions. *Typical tuk-tuk maneuvers.*

The hijacked truck veered into the ramp of an elevated expressway, still under construction. The construction workers shouted, ran after them, and blocked access to the ramp. The tuk-tuk went under the expressway and weaved around construction supplies to resume the chase.

They came out from under the expressway just in time to see their hijacked truck exit the ramp and turn into a side street. Alan pointed the driver that way. Two minutes later the tuk-tuk turned into the same street, but Alan saw only an empty roadway ahead.

They drove down the street, searched but didn't find anything. Alan said, "This is too far. We've got to turn around, search the laneways we passed."

Leng agreed and translated for the driver. They turned around and stopped at the first lane entrance they came to. Leng jumped off, ran in, then returned shaking his head. They went to the next lane where Leng looked again with no success. At the third laneway, Alan jumped off, ran in, and found nothing, but in the next one he saw the truck. He ran back to summon the others.

Sakda and Leng hopped off, and Alan dismissed the tuk-tuk. The driver grinned and zoomed away fast, as if he was worried they'd change their minds about paying a small fortune for such a short ride.

They headed up the alley. A thug popped out from a doorway ahead of them. Two more appeared from the street behind, and yet another appeared farther up the alley. One man stayed back to block the exit to the street. The other three wore *mae sawks*—wooden clubs strapped to the forearm. They closed in and launched their assault.

Leng ducked, and the mae sawk just missed his head. Sakda seemed to succumb to a blow, his attacker relaxed, and Sakda hit back, stunning his opponent. Alan charged forward and knocked his assailant down and out with a flying kick. *My jungle fighting practice paid off.* He intervened on Leng's behalf to partly deflect a major blow. Leng's attacker went after him, and they fought to a draw until Leng recovered and rejoined the struggle.

Their opponent backed off, looked at his losing team, then promptly fled the alleyway. The other attackers abandoned the fight and followed him.

Alan was a little giddy with his fighting success. "Neighborhood watch?"

"A trap," Leng said.

They ran to the truck. "More like a warning," Alan said. "Harry left mae sawks behind, not guns."

Sakda opened the driver's door and screamed out when Kapono's dead body fell into his arms. Shocked silence was soon followed by angry curses; they'd lost their snake-charming jungle brother. Sakda put Kapono's body down. "Barang get warning. Khmer not so lucky."

Alan grabbed an iron bar and pried open the back door of the truck. It was completely empty. He hung his head in despair. "They must've had another truck waiting here."

The three men sat in silence. Alan's voice firmed up. "For what it's worth, I'll report Kapono's murder to the police." The notorious Cambodian police were usually too busy generating income to properly investigate crime. "And I'll arrange for his body to go back to Maran." He gestured to Leng and Sakda. "Take the truck back to the hotel. I'll get the Land Cruiser after I deal with this and meet you there."

They hot-wired the truck to get it started and drove away, while Alan called the police on his phone.

Around the laneway several people emerged from hiding spots to watch the truck leave with the two Cambodians while Alan stayed behind. The spectators whispered and surreptitiously looked at each other's phones. They huddled together, away from Alan, perhaps never sure which barang can be trusted. When the police arrived, they disappeared.

Unexpected Ally

Alan nursed a beer in the posh lobby bar of the Rosewood Hotel and tapped languidly on his phone. *Ripped off again. Another dead worker.*

The Bataris sat next to him, huddled together over coffee cups. Leng paced the floor. Sakda looked out of place; he stared at the fish in the large aquarium behind the reception desk.

The fancy elevator doors opened, and Yuying marched into the lobby; heads turned and conversation faltered. She acknowledged Sakda then stopped right in front of Alan (who was still engaged with his phone) looking stern. Alan eventually registered her presence and looked up.

"Hypocrite," Yuying said.

"Huh?"

"Don't 'huh' me, you slimeball."

Sakda and Leng were gobsmacked by the confrontation. Everyone in the lobby held their breath and watched. Alan stood up. "What are you—?"

"'Treaty writer breaks own treaty,'" she mimicked. "'It goes against all my principles.'"

Now Alan got it; he gently took Yuying's elbow and led her to a quiet corner. He waited for the attention to die off. "Okay, I give up." He raised his hands in surrender. "I'm a hypocrite." Then he remembered Betty's photos from the Sora Bar; his face turned stony. "Now what the hell is going on? How can you work with scum like Harry Dunlap?"

"How—?" Caught briefly off guard, she recovered. "He hired me to sort out a bunch of Grace agarwood. Mostly plantation oil," she said. Her voice turned sharp. "But guess what?"

Alan forgot about the photos. Harry had been busy with his

stolen stash, had even recruited Yuying to help. He slumped. *The treasure is long gone.* "You were right, I needed it to finish my research." He raised his head. "But it's not from clear-cuts."

Yuying snorted out a hollow laugh. "I remember someone else saying that."

"I was there! In the jungle. I have video. We found an old fallen tree."

"Oh, that justifies everything."

"But Batar is desperate. Maran needs the money." He hung his head. "My workers are getting killed. I've let everyone down."

"Yup."

"And my name is mud." He sat down, completely deflated.

Yuying stared at Alan and came to a decision. "There's a way to fix this."

Alan looked up, not sure if he could be hopeful.

She raised her eyebrows. "It might destroy *my* reputation, but I'll help you recover the treasure." Alan came alert, and she added, "And I'll keep my mouth shut."

"In exchange for?" He was again wary.

"I have a list." She smiled mischievously.

***

Alone together in the hotel suite, Yuying and Alan were suddenly awkward. Yuying took a small vial from her handbag, opened it, and rubbed some oil on Alan's neck. He recognized the scent and opened his mouth to speak, but Yuying stopped him with her finger on his lips. She opened her blouse and pulled him toward the bed.

PING PING.

Alan apologized, took out his phone, and read a text. It was from Kareem.

- Nazneen condition critical.

He collapsed on the bed.

Yuying gently took his phone and read the text. "The princess?" she said softly.

Alan stared right through Yuying, then slowly focused on her. "We're too late."

"No," she said, fiercely determined. "We'll get it back."

Alan slowly came round and acknowledged Yuying's support. He straightened his shoulders and stood up, his mind made up. "Okay, let's get started."

He made for the door, while Yuying sighed, rebuttoned her blouse, and followed him out.

***

Yuying was in the passenger seat of the old truck, and Fan drove. Alan and Leng were in the back. Fan parked directly across from a blue warehouse. It sat in the middle of a row of small warehouses, each behind secure fences with gates and guard posts. Yuying pointed. "In there. That's Harry's truck parked at the side."

Alan addressed Fan and Yuying. "Watch the big door. Bring the truck in as soon as it opens right up."

Sakda came up the street disguised as a soup vendor. He pushed a cart with a pot of hot broth and all the fixings for fresh soup. A truck with giant speakers came from the other direction. It blasted a Muay Thai boxing promotion, parked down near the pink warehouse, and kept blaring. A small payment to the driver had easily arranged this distraction after they'd paid a slightly bigger bribe to borrow

Sakda's soup cart. Sakda approached the guard at the blue warehouse gate.

Alan said to Leng, "You take care of the guard, I'll go straight in."

The guard frowned at Sakda. Sakda stayed cool and offered him a taste. Alan sweated bullets. Finally the guard opened the gate and let Sakda through. He pushed the cart to the warehouse and squeezed under the partly open door.

Leng and Alan jumped out of the truck and rushed to the gate before it closed. Alan caught it just in time and pushed it back open. The guard got up and reached for his gun, but Leng plowed into him before he could take aim. The two men struggled for control of the gun; the guard was winning until Alan came back to the rescue. Two on one, they subdued the guard, tied him up, and looked to see if they'd attracted any attention. Nope, the Muay Thai truck was blaring, and their plan was working. They ran into the warehouse.

Harry and Samphy lay facedown on the floor. Sakda casually pointed a semiautomatic rifle at them and tasted the soup.

Alan took the gun from Sakda, kept it pointed at the bad guys, and chuckled. "How wrong I was!"

"Yeah, you shouldn'ta messed with me," Harry said.

Leng pushed the warehouse door all the way open as Alan replied, "No, I just couldn't imagine I'd ever be glad to see you again." Harry looked baffled; Alan continued. "And that's simply because you took something that doesn't belong to you … and I need it back."

The truck came into the warehouse; Alan smiled at and thanked Yuying. He pointed to the stolen goods. "It's all here! Let's get this stuff to the airport."

They loaded the truck. Alan looked back at Harry, shook his head, and said to Yuying, "We should kill him."

Harry went pale.

"Too bad it goes against all my principles." Alan looked rueful.

Yuying grabbed Alan's ear. "Scoundrel." It almost turned into a caress.

Harry noticed. "Hey, lovebirds, you can't hide. You have no idea what you're up against."

Alan ignored him but looked at Leng and Sakda and grinned. "Call the Yee Shing Tong?"

Harry and Samphy both flinched. Not many survived an encounter with the notorious Chinese mafia gang.

***

Alan, Leng, and Sakda transferred the cargo from the truck to the Batari Airways freight containers at the dusty windswept airfield. The fancy white limo pulled up, the two Bataris got out, thanked Alan, and provided customs with the export paperwork. The containers were loaded onto the plane.

Alan hugged Leng and Sakda. He embraced and kissed Yuying.

"Don't go," she said.

"I have to."

"You miss her that much, huh?"

"There are hundreds of sick Bataris," Alan said. "I have to make sure it arrives."

"No. You. Don't. It's risky, more exposure."

"Overexposed already. Please be patient; I'll be back in a few days. We regroup at the plantation. Go with Leng and Sakda, and wait for me there."

Alan boarded the plane.

Briefly Back in Batar

Alan slept soundly on the luxurious aircraft, for the full seven-hour flight to the Arabian Gulf. Kareem met his plane, and together they rushed the cargo to the loading dock of the Batar General Hospital, then went in the front door and entered the bright hospital corridor.

Kareem's arrival should have been a big event, where everyone made way and deferred to their king. On this day, chaos reigned; they threaded their way through crowds of nurses, doctors, orderlies, and patients on stretchers attached to IV drips. They found and chatted with Dr. Armand, dressed in spotless hospital whites. She escorted them past open doors where more sick people filled the rooms.

The doctor had an angelic face and spoke with a thick French accent. "Yes, you brought the oil just in time. We ran out last night. The worst cases are all here ... responding well. We're so grateful."

They arrived at a closed door; Dr. Armand gestured at the little window. Alan looked into the room and gasped.

"Yes, our sickest patient," she said.

They went in. Nazneen lay on the bed, pale and frail, dwarfed by the big machines attached to her by numerous tubes and wires.

"Oh, Nazneen." Alan was crushed.

"We induced a coma, to give the agarwood therapy a chance to work."

"Prognosis?"

"Uncertain. We increase the dose every day. The body tolerates, eventually thrives on high doses ... unlike chemotherapy."

Big Pharma Fights Back

Quentin T. Wilkes, CEO of SpringenRx Corporation, was a happy man. He'd triumphed last night at the PhRMA convention (Pharmaceutical Research and Manufacturers of America) and then woken up next to the beautiful, powerful woman who had been so helpful to his company. His seduction of FDA Commissioner Paula Bondwell had taken a while, but he had no regrets.

His company was about to take a big leap forward after a bad couple of years. Finding agarwood had saved his ass. It held incredible potential for healing. But it was too hard to control and profit from a tree. He'd developed his new drugs from the synthetic agarwood they'd patented. And convinced the government that natural agarwood was dangerous, while their concoctions were safe. The drug business was about to be disrupted big time, and he was going to be the main disruptor and beneficiary.

Wilkes just needed to clear up a few lingering, inconvenient issues. First and foremost that meant silencing that pesky scientist, Alan Grace. He opened his CIA-provided teleconferencing software and called Humboldt at the US embassy in Phnom Penh. Humboldt answered in voice mode.

"Turn on the video," Wilkes said.

Humboldt's face appeared onscreen. He looked like crap.

"You said Grace was dead."

"*Harry* said Grace was dead," Humboldt replied.

"Then 'the local cops will take care of it.'"

"Harry thought—"

"Now sightings in Phnom Penh and Batar."

"Yes." Humboldt gave up.

"Harry is useless."

***

"Ya think?" Harry, mean and mad, loomed in the doorway; the fresh scars from his encounter with the Yee Shing Tong glimmered in the harsh office light. Humboldt cowered. Even Wilkes, safely far away, looked wary.

"Grace got away, but I'll have access to all his data, even the most recent."

"You have the data?" Wilkes became alert. "Get it to my research team, right aw—"

"Already working on it." Or at least I've got Humboldt working on a way to get past the fingerprint security.

"Okay." Wilkes sounded somewhat placated. "What about Grace?"

"I have a plan. To neutralize him."

"The rape scenario? That sure whacked WikiLeaks."

"We tried. He's too clean."

"What about all that perfume stuff, those models…?"

Harry shook his head.

Wilkes leered. "He has some hot students…" Another head shake from Harry. "The princess?"

"He's either been a gentleman and Mr. Discreet … or he's still a fucking virgin." Harry got an unwanted vision of Yuying caressing Alan while Alan sneered at him. Harry frowned, shook it off, and brandished a brown portfolio. "I sent this to Greenpeace. Proof that Grace broke the convention, the same one he wrote. And"—he tossed a blue portfolio to Humboldt—"Interpol got my other valentine."

Humboldt's eyes widened, and he nodded and smiled. "A murder in Phnom Penh … a dead cop in the jungle."

"Either one works." Harry grinned. "We ain't fussy."

Back to Square One

Alan Grace and King Kareem walked down the hospital corridor. It was even more crowded than before. Kareem probed insistently. "Are you sure? It's over ten million dollars."

"Yes. Pay me for the plantation oil, but the big check goes into the Maran Trust account."

Kareem shook his head in quiet disbelief. "You kept enough oil, for your research?"

"Yes. I finished it, the main phase. Hope it's not too late. Got to get the information out before SpringenRx shuts us down."

"How can they—?"

"They've got the key to my data, maybe the data itself by now. They'll release an expensive synthetic version. Block the natural stuff."

Kareem chuckled. "Block the … It's only the foundation scent in all great fragrances. And the key ingredient in the best incense!"

"Okay, they won't touch that side … yet."

Kareem frowned skeptically.

"Okay, maybe never. But agarwood is virtually unknown in the West, and the media machine is very effective. They'll demonize it and stop the medicinal products by placing them on Schedule One. Big Pharma, the FDA, and the DEA—joined at the hip."

Kareem and Alan reached Nazneen's door, opened it, and entered the room. They joined Dr. Armand at Nazneen's bedside, and Kareem grasped her limp hand. Dr. Armand said, "She is stable now, even improving a little. But…"

"But?" Alan asked.

"Nazneen, like many, needs massive amounts of the oil."

"Two barrels, *ten million dollars* isn't enough?"

"There are over two hundred patients in this hospital alone; more every day."

"How much m—? When will you run out?" Alan was already thinking ahead.

"A few weeks, but … the story of this cure has leaked."

"How so?" Kareem asked.

"We are getting requests from all over the Gulf. Everywhere downwind of the war is reporting outbreaks."

"How big?"

"Massif. Milliers— thousands of cases."

"I've got to go," Alan said.

Kareem and Dr. Armand looked at him.

Alan ran to the door then turned back, his gaze on Nazneen. "I need to get all the agarwood plantations, everywhere, on track producing high quality oil." He left the room.

"Godspeed," Kareem whispered. Then he jumped up, followed Alan, and arranged for his jet to take Alan directly to Phnom Penh. He'd had a driver meet him there, and Alan was back in Maran in record time, just twelve hours later.

The Grace Disgrace

Back in the plantation lab, Alan, Yuying, Betty, and Leng lounged around a table full of dirty dishes and half-eaten food. Sakda sat quietly by the window. When Tevy came in to clear away the mess, Leng and Betty jumped up to help her. Alan toyed with his new satellite phone, the latest model he'd acquired in Batar. He was frustrated with the upgraded device—he'd liked his old, simpler model that Rithy had taken from him. Betty came back, sat beside him, and took the phone. She soon figured out the new device, showed Alan the more intricate features, then took it back again. "I'll upload your contacts."

"Thanks. I guess you can add my old number…"

"Under Rithy." Betty nodded and smiled and took it to the annex.

Alan shrugged. The ceiling fan was the only movement or sound for a few minutes until Yuying spoke up. "They'll pin the smuggling rap on you."

Alan stared through her. "Don't care. Too many lives at stake."

"One in particular."

"We've got to go public, share all my grow-and-prep knowledge." He spoke faster. "And we've got to tell the world about the medical applications before SpringenRx can injunction us." Even faster: "I've got to get access to my data again, I—"

"Harry doesn't have the fob anymore." Betty got his attention as she came into the main lab. She gave the new phone back to him. "But I think I know who has it now. I've arranged to meet him, a few days from now in Phnom Penh … a hot date!"

"Okay, if we get the facts out we can fight the lies," Alan said.

"I'll be ready to *publish*."

Alan had another brief vision of porn sites. "Just get me access to the data and wait for my word." Then he softened his voice. "It's got to be foolproof. We need a better lead for the story. Something that will make it go viral when they try and kill it."

Betty nodded and went back to work.

Alan turned around and said to Sakda and Leng, "Please get some samples ready." He looked at Yuying. "Can you go to…?" He was improvising. "To Battambang and book a meeting room at the Mae Ping?"

"A press conference … in Battambang?"

Battambang was the closest city to Maran. It *was* a charming provincial capital with the best-preserved colonial architecture in the country. A hub of international journalists it was not.

"Okay, the Rosewood in Phnom Penh."

"That's more like it," she said. They sprang into action.

***

 Yuying watched a muted TV and enjoyed the luxury at the Rosewood Hotel. The pleasure faded; a news channel was hyping a breaking story, "The Grace Disgrace." Her cell rang, and she answered, "Y. Li"

"Oh, fragrant Li, I'm on my way." Alan's voice.

"You haven't heard? Where are you?"

"Heard what?"

"An international warrant." Yuying read from the TV. "Your picture is everywhere. You're wanted."

"For what?"

"The international warrant is for smuggling," Yuying said.

"Big deal."

"And there's a local warrant for murder."

"What the fuck?"

"Kapono."

"But *I* reported that."

"And a dead cop in the jungle."

"I have video evidence to clear me on that one."

"Not at the moment. Genius messed up." Yuying was pointing out that due to Betty's elaborate security scheme, everything in cloud storage was inaccessible until they recovered the fob. Yuying saw more headlines on TV. "Wait, more evidence. The—"

"Gotta go." The call ended.

***

Alan did a U-turn along a dusty road, hit the gas pedal, then got Google News on his cell and confirmed that he was indeed the main story. He cursed, pulled into a row of primitive shops, and saw a farmer coming. He grabbed the phone and charger, removed them from their waterproof pouch, got out, bowed slightly, and offered them to the farmer. Baffled but grateful, he accepted Alan's gift and touched the screen—it lit up with the Google News story. He did a double take when he recognized the photos of Alan.

Alan ran into the shack advertising cell phones and came out a few minutes later with a new phone. He put it in the waterproof pouch, clipped it to the dashboard holder, and set it on hands-free. He tapped in a number and pulled away.

RING RING.

"Hello," Leng answered.

"Where are you?"

"Alan? They look to arrest you."

"I know. Where are you?"

"Maran. Police are here. I don't believe—"

"Later. Where's Sakda?"

"Looking for chief."

Alan sighed. "Khmer Loeu don't do extradition ... okay, meet me at Xanadu."

**

Harry and Samphy followed the GPS app on Harry's phone. They reached a peaceful farm, approached a hut from opposite sides, and raised their weapons. Harry yelled out, "Police! Come out."

Samphy repeated it in Khmer.

A loud wail from a baby stopped them; they lowered their weapons. Harry yanked the door open and saw the farmer with Alan's cell. His scars turned a livid red, and he grabbed the cell while a woman shrieked and cowered behind the man, clutching her baby.

**

Betty rushed up to the hilltop clearing, well beyond the Grace plantation and found Sakda quietly waiting. He had hoisted a bright yellow rag to the top of a tall tree to signal the Khmer Loeu that he needed to get a message to Rithy. Though it always worked, it could take a while. Perhaps she didn't have his patience, but she did have technology on her side. She pulled out the new satellite phone; Sakda laughed. She clicked on a number and tried to hand the phone to Sakda as it rang, but he looked the other way.

RING RING.

Rithy's face appeared, almost too young to match his mature

baritone voice that filled the air. "Hello."

"Wow, huh, Chief Rithy, ah … ah. Hi, Chief, I'm Betty." Suddenly preening and awkward. *Was Sakda amused?* She turned her back to him.

"Hello to Betty."

"Nice to, ah… meet you. Umm…" She recovered. "I'm here with Sakda." She turned, put the phone on speaker, and aimed the cam at him.

Sakda and Rithy had barely exchanged greetings before Betty aimed the phone back at her own face. "Alan needs your help, the police are chasing him, they think—"

"I understand," Rithy said. "Police make big lies. No problem, Khmer Loeu can help."

Rithy gave detailed instructions on where to rendezvous, then laughed off Betty's effusive thanks with a bow. "My pleasure," he said, winked, and asked for Sakda.

Betty handed the phone over as her breathing returned to normal. She enjoyed listening to their fluent conversation even though she didn't understand the words. Rithy's English was better than she'd expected, while Sakda seemed happy to rely on his limited vocabulary. In their native tongues they sounded like different people.

***

Alan arrived at Xanadu and tried to ignore the inebriated people cheering on the rope swingers who dropped into the river. He went into the hut, ordered coffee, and surveyed the more subdued crowd languishing inside. They ignored each other, faces locked to their own little screens. Alan got a view of one—his photo captioned with "Fugitive."

Around the room, more and more people began to notice that

the man pictured in news alerts on their phones was actually among them. They eyeballed Alan, rechecked their phones, and began to gossip and point. Two young women moved away from Alan. The bartender put down his cell and tapped on a remote control. In the crowded hut, the scents became a stench.

The big TV got switched from a reggae video to a news site. It showed a photo of Alan in academic garb while the newsreader pretended to be excited. "Dr. Grace resigned while under investigation for academic fraud."

Next, the TV showed headshots of Kapono and Kosal, the dead cop from the Teuk Vet incident. "But the smuggling and fraud charges are just the tip of the iceberg. Alan Grace is wanted for murder. And it doesn't stop there. Grace is accused of supporting terrorism; it seems his profits are allegedly funding al-Qaeda." The TV then showed gruesome and totally unrelated photos of bomb victims in Pakistan.

The patrons and staff gathered under the TV, glancing in disgust at Alan, the perfect villain, while they argued about what to do. "Call the cops," one of them said, then looked startled and dropped his joint.

Everyone laughed but Alan. On the TV, Alan accepted an award while the chyrons rolled:

"Award winning scientist gone rogue?"

"Wanted for murder!"

"Weird twist: UN adviser breaks his own treaties."

Then Keat Chhon filled the screen. "Yes, Cambodian police are investigating these crimes."

Reporters yelled at Keat, "Where is Alan Grace?" "Do you have the murderer?" "Are you protecting a terrorist?"

"We are acting on an international warrant and expect to apprehend the fugitive soon." He turned his back and left the podium while the reporters yelled more queries.

Alan took his coffee and went back outside, but even the crowd out there was sobering up as they caught on to the story. Alan didn't like their ugly stares and accusations; their stale odors were worse.

He fingered his amulet then cheered up when he saw Leng speeding in on a motorcycle. Leng braked hard, parked, and ran across the deck to Alan. He grabbed Alan's arm, dragged him to the side of the deck above the river, and pointed to a possible escape route along the cliff.

A police 4x4 arrived and parked next to Leng's bike. The party was suddenly over; people hid their bongs and joints and slipped away while Harry and Samphy got out of the vehicle.

Alan didn't like Leng's idea for an escape route and shook his head. "This way." He grabbed the swing-rope and gave it to Leng. "You go first." Leng backed up while Alan pointed to the rocks. "Watch out."

Leng leaped and swung out but didn't quite let go in time; he dropped and barely missed the rocks.

Alan gulped at the near miss; Harry reached the deck. The rope swung back. Alan grabbed it, ran, and leaped off the deck, then splashed down near Leng just right—well past the rocks. They swam hard and fast, taking advantage of the current.

***

Harry ran to the edge of the deck and shot at them. He missed. Leng and Alan disappeared downriver under the overhanging canopy. Samphy tapped his arm, pointing to the spectators taking videos, and Harry put his gun away. The two men huddled to discuss their next move.

A Day-Glo purple truck, the same one Harry had followed across the border, came down the road and parked outside the hut. The paragliding equipment was gone; the truck was empty. The blond barang couple emerged from the truck and carried on a loud argument in thick accents, oblivious to the drama at the river. "I showed you how to lock them up," the man shouted.

"I did exactly as you ordered!" his partner shouted back. "Besides, you didn't park where I told you to."

Moon Quest

The half-moon shed an eerie light over the riverside clearing. Leng, Sakda, and Alan discussed their predicament in hushed tones but eventually fell silent. Betty and Rithy were deep into their first face-to-face encounter. Betty showed Rithy some additional features he could use on his satellite phone. Rithy told Betty about the refuge where he would hide Alan. Their physical attraction was obvious, perhaps enhanced on another level—witch to warlock?

Sakda finally broke it up. "Time to go."

Betty grinned and backed away. She said to Alan, "I'm going to Phnom Penh tomorrow. I'll get the fob."

Alan gave her a hug. Rithy got in the stern of his kayak. Alan tried to hug Sakda, hugged Leng, climbed into the bow, and pushed off. They waved and paddled away, up the river, gliding along in the soft moonlight and passing dark jungle on both sides. Alan said, "Thank you, Chief. Again."

"Thank you for good kayak," replied Rithy. His English improved at every use.

Alan sighed; Leng had thanked him for exactly the same thing. But he appreciated the gratitude, especially as the kayak was neither stolen nor gifted. It was salvage, recovered by the Khmer Loeu after he'd lost it at the waterfalls. Rithy was young, perhaps younger than Alan. He seemed wise beyond his years.

"Sakda say you are famous barang."

"More like *in*famous now."

"Tell me."

"I helped write some treaties, got a big prize … Now I'm accused of smuggling, framed for murder—remember the dead cop at Teuk Vet? Legally and professionally, I'm toast."

"Il-le-gal pro-fes-sion-al toast?"

"With jam!" Alan laughed. "Do I belong with the bad guys, the smugglers?"

"Belong with Khmer Loeu … for now."

"Sure, 'bungle in the jungle' while planet Earth falls apart."

"No. Planet Earth like agarwood tree. First get sick then fight back, get stronger."

"The planet's infected all right. But where's the mold-killing resin to save it?"

"You, people same like you … and people same like Khmer Loeu."

***

Betty looked stunning and sexy. There was nothing demure about the new outfit she'd put together at the boutique next door to Salvatore Ferragamo. She liked the clothes, but what had really clinched the purchase was the brand name: Maje, the French version of the word *mage*. She'd really liked it when Alan had bestowed that title on her.

Humboldt relished the envious leers of the other men at the Sora Bar, telling spy stories to impress her. He obviously assumed she was just a beautiful bimbo, well beyond his usual power of attraction. A large tip had secured the best table for both privacy and view. She sipped her exotic cocktail and watched Humboldt drain his drink. He set it down next to three empties and reordered. A new drink arrived, and the empties were whisked away. He ran out of things to say…

"That must have taken a lot of courage." Betty "picked up the ball."

"Just part of the job."

"So modest," she said and began to detail the wonders of Southeast Asian temples. Humboldt hung on every word, perhaps never before realizing his keen interest in religious iconography. She gave a lengthy description of the vast Angkor Wat complex, leaned over the table, exposed even more cleavage, and touched his arm. Keeping him focused on her face and low neckline, she poured some liquid into his drink, went on with her story. He gulped down half his drink as she described the sunset from the hill at Phnom Bakheng. "But I won't ever go back."

"Why not?" Humboldt uncrossed his eyes at this surprise.

"It was so crowded. And I've had my turn. There are so many visitors to Angkor Wat now that the site is being damaged." Betty took a sip of her own drink through the straw and then threw the straw down with a flourish. She clinked glasses. "Bottoms up." They drained their glasses. Betty waited for a few minutes, then got up. "Let's go."

Humboldt stared back up at her with his mouth agape. She signaled the waitress for the bill.

"What the f—?" Humboldt seemed confused about the extent of his inebriation until the waitress brought the long bill. He glanced at the list of drinks, grinned, and handed over two hundred dollars. "Keep the change."

"Come on, we've had way too much." Betty slurred her words slightly.

She led him inside to the elevator and then down to the car park. She found the parking ticket in his pocket and gave it to the valet. The valet handed her the keys and pointed to the car, close by in a prime spot next to a Lamborghini. Cars with diplomatic plates got special treatment.

She helped Humboldt into the passenger seat and then got behind the wheel. They left the underground car park, cruised out onto the boulevard, and nosed into the slow traffic. While Humboldt lolled next to her, she drove the short distance to the US embassy, lowered the window, and gave the marine guard in the gatehouse her twenty-carat smile. "I'm the designated driver after all." The marine grinned and waved them through, looking like he wished he could be

Humboldt.

Betty pulled into the car park and roused Humboldt, half-carried him past the residence door, and used his ID card to swipe them into the deserted main building of the embassy. She sat him down in a comfy office chair on rollers and went to find the technical communications office. It was close by in the small embassy.

She rolled him quietly to the tech room and again swiped the ID card, but this door wouldn't open. She noticed a faint beeping and tiny flashing light: a fingerprint scanner prompting for input. She gently lifted Humboldt's hand.

He roused, opened one eye, and grinned at her. Betty leaned in, grinned back, then slowly closed her eyes. Humboldt dozed back off with a smile; she positioned his fingers on the scanner, and the door slid open.

***

Betty barreled through the plantation gate on her motorcycle, parked abruptly in front of Leng, and yanked off her helmet. Leng and some helpers were fixing the mess from the latest police raid. They'd turned the place upside down, made threats to get answers about Alan's current location, then smashed up some huts in frustration. Betty was out of breath; it was a long ride from Phnom Penh.

"You okay?" Leng asked. He sounded low.

"Got the fob. We can connect Alan to his data. And I found the lead … to launch our story. I think it's foolproof, a guaranteed media circus." Leng looked less forlorn. "I need the sat phone."

Leng pulled the phone out of his pack and handed it to Betty. She selected Rithy's number.

RING RING.

Rithy's face appeared, and his deep voice answered, "Hello."

"Hi, Chief." Betty sounded confident. Her heart fluttered.

"Hello to Betty."

"Nice to see you again. Umm…"

"You want Alan." He gave her a big smile, then disappeared. She got a glimpse of a primitive hut before Alan appeared on the small screen, bearded, tanned, and relaxed.

"Hey, what's up?"

"Got the fob."

"There is a God."

"And I'm working on the Phnom Penh murder, so I offered a reward, already got a response. I think I can get videos of the cargo transfer and the fight. I've only seen one so far, but … that was quite the kick. Hey, boss, when did you become a ninja?"

"You think the videos will help?" Alan looked anxious.

"Absolutely! Enough to clear you."

Alan relaxed a bit. "Kareem has offered me asylum."

"If you can make it to the Batari embassy in Phnom Penh. Sorry, it already leaked."

Alan flinched, and his face turned hard. "We've gotta get the story out."

"Hey, I solved that problem too. Got a media torpedo with a fuse! A setup that will guarantee us a story."

"Okay, what?"

"SpringenRx and the FDA are sleeping together."

"Like that's news."

"No. I mean really. Really rutting! CEO Quentin Wilkes is romancing the FDA Commissioner, Paula Bondwell."

"Explains a lot." He was starting to share her enthusiasm.

"And the proof! I decrypted their private message stream. Talk about porn."

"Quite the fuse. Hook 'em on sex."

"Then blow their whole wad—"

"Into a hurricane of headlines." They grinned at each other.

Alan thanked her profusely then mock-commanded, "Light the fuse!"

Betty saluted. "Yessir!" She turned serious. "Be careful."

"Let me talk to Leng," Alan said. Betty handed the phone to Leng.

They exchanged greetings, then Alan said, "Drive to Chamnar, call us from there. Use the tuk-tuk."

"Huh? Old freight tuk-tuk?" Leng said.

"Yeah, its the only thing we've got that can handle the trails past Chamnar and still carry two of us out of there."

***

Quentin Wilkes drank red wine; Paula Bondwell poured herself a glass. They relaxed in naked postcoital bliss in front of a silent TV in a Chicago hotel room.

Oops. The TV showed the two of them posing for an awkward publicity photo over the breaking-story headline "PharmaGate." Wilkes grabbed the remote and turned on the sound. "…and what appears to be evidence of an affair between Quentin T. Wilkes, the SpringenRx CEO, and Paula Bondwell, Commissioner of the FDA."

Bondwell pulled the sheet up in a reflexive attempt at modesty and frowned at Wilkes, who'd spilled his wine and was whimpering like a wounded puppy. The newsreader continued to torture them. "More PharmaGate shockers: NDA questioned about special exemptions and expedited approvals for new SpringenRx medications."

***

A tall, slim, anonymous motorcycle rider pulled into a Phnom Penh laneway. The rider stopped and took off her dust mask and helmet. Betty had found the location of the ambush. Her phone chirped, she read a message, and yelled out loud, "PharmaGate?" Then she grinned. *We made 'Gate' status.*

Her outburst attracted attention; several people started video capture on their phones. More folks arrived in the alley. Betty smiled, showed photos of Harry. One stepped forward and identified himself as the source of the video she'd already received. She glanced at his phone, gave him twenty dollars.

Three others got excited at the sight of the cash and jostled their way in to show her their video clips. Shot from different windows along the alleyway, the videos were a little choppy and confusing, but taken together they painted a clear picture of what had happened: Harry and Samphy arriving, transferring the cargo, taking off in their own truck. Kapono's body was clearly visible, slumped over the dash of the hijacked truck.

They also had video of Alan's group arriving and fighting off Harry's goons, as well as a clip showing Sakda finding Kapono. She shared her email address and gave out money as her phone pinged with their incoming videos.

***

Alan squatted in Rithy's hut. Not only bearded and tanned, his muscled body was painted and almost naked. He was stony faced; the asylum offer had leaked. He had to get past an army now.

Rithy noticed his distress. He got up, checked out Alan's shoulders, biceps, trunk, and legs and nodded approval. Alan had become a warrior; a meek biologist no more. "Strong body," he said.

"I'm ready?"

"Almost ready. Body ready. Now, need strong spirit. Time for Moon Quest."

Alan looked up at the full moon. Rithy chanted, poured some oil into a little cup, and held it up to Alan's face.

Alan sniffed. "Drink that? Ten thousand dollars, down my throat?"

"No. No dollars here."

Rithy took out a beehive-shaped plastic squeeze bottle of Beehive Honey. Alan flinched at seeing the modern anomaly so deep in the jungle. Rithy squeezed some honey into the cup, mixed it up, and handed it to Alan.

"But—"

"Gift. From jungle. Drink."

Alan touched his amulet then shrugged and complied. After a few minutes, he closed his eyes and felt himself rise. He opened his eyes, looked back down at Rithy and his own body, then went up through the roof and into the clouds.

He soon emerged into a strange landscape above the clouds and saw a stone courthouse that dominated the bleak scene. Two foo-dog lions guarded the entrance, one on each side. These foo-dogs were alive, snarling, and both had Harry's face. Alan ignored them. He passed through and walked up into the courthouse.

Inside the courtroom, Keat Chhon sat high up behind a judge's bench. He'd donned a white judicial wig and was banging a gavel.

Alan joined the defense table, headed by Kareem. Behind Kareem sat Leng, Sakda, Betty, Yuying, and Chief Rithy. Alan stared at Harry over at the prosecution bench.

The courtroom spectators all looked familiar: plantation workers; Khmer Loeu warriors; perfumed models; the hapless governess; the inspector and his new companion; Yuying's bodyguard, Fan; Tevy; soldiers; party hut people; Kapono's ghost; and the Maran villagers.

Saffron-robed monks entered the courtroom quietly chanting. They carried smoking incense and filled the jury box. The rich aroma of agarwood, tinged with a slight floral scent, filled the air. Alan's nose twitched.

"Defendant will rise," Judge Keat said.

Already standing, Alan floated up off the floor a bit. Yuying rolled her eyes and yanked him down.

Prosecutor Harry read an indictment. "Charges include poaching, smuggling, rogue research, murder, terrorism, and"—he struggled with the final item on the list—"breaking hearts?" He recovered. "First prosecution witness is…" He screwed up his face, even more puzzled. "Princess Nazneen?"

Healthy and beautiful, Nazneen glided down the aisle past a sea of shocked faces. She took the stand, looked lovingly at Alan, and recited:

"To pass the test

Just do your best.

Gift from forest

Completes the quest."

Flying Again

Rithy watched Alan as he returned to reality in the little hut.

"I'm ready," Alan said.

"Okay." Rithy enveloped him in a big hug but cut it short when they heard gunfire. "We go."

Rithy grabbed his satellite phone and clipped it to his belt. They left the hut, ran through the trees, and out onto a clearing at the top of a steep hill where the west wind was strong and the view opened up to the green valleys far below. Shouts, shots, and other sounds of conflict came from the trail in the trees below them.

Rithy went behind a rocky hump, pulled some branches aside, and disappeared into a narrow opening. He pulled out a paraglider pack and a helmet.

"Unbelievable." Alan laughed.

"Yes. Donation from ecotourist."

"A donation?" Alan said with a snort. Then his expression changed. "It's been ten years since I sailed!"

Rithy laughed and clipped a cam to the helmet. Alan turned it on and put on the helmet while soldiers came out of the forest below. Rithy said, "Fast quick." He helped Alan into the glider harness and readied the sail.

Alan turned into the wind but stopped and fingered his amulet. "You okay?"

Rithy laughed but urgently gestured for Alan to get going.

Alan shook the harness and pulled the sail up a bit to catch the wind. Rithy copied him with the other side; the sail billowed in the breeze. Alan ran forward down the hill until the sail fully caught the wind. The first soldiers reached the top of the hill and headed their way. Alan was still running, but his feet had left the ground; the paraglider lifted him into the air.

Rithy ran behind the rock hump, into the hidden cave, and pulled the branches back behind him to cover the entrance. He grabbed the satellite phone and tapped Alan's number.

RING RING.

"Hello, this is Leng."

"Alan come. Now."

"Okay," Leng said.

They ended the call.

Rithy heard loud bangs; he hoped the soldiers were bad shots.

***

Alan sailed out and got beyond the soldiers' range. He grinned, high on adrenaline; his paragliding skills had come back to him. He soared away, enjoying the alpine scents and the bird's-eye views.

He saw Leng in a clearing below, flashing a little mirror. He swooped down but couldn't resist a final lift back up to the sky when he caught an updraft. Leng stopped flashing the mirror, put the satellite phone in the old freight tuk-tuk, and waited while looking impatient. Alan swooped back and forth with confidence then finally landed gracefully right next to Leng. They laughed, hugged, then packed up the glider, threw it in the tuk-tuk, and took off. Alan drove while Leng sat in the cargo bucket holding the pack.

They left the clearing, bumped along till they found a road out of the jungle and heard another vehicle. A police 4x4 had pulled out of a hiding spot in the trees. It followed fast, soon gaining on them.

They could see Harry riding shotgun, next to Samphy behind the wheel. Shots rang out and one bullet hit their tuk-tuk. Alan sped up and the old engine complained. He turned hard right. He'd found a shortcut—a footpath on a narrow ridge between two sunken rice fields. The tuk-tuk barely fit on the narrow path, but somehow Alan got to the far side of the field. He turned right. Now back on the road, they'd left the 4x4 well behind. It had to follow the road all the way around the fields.

They entered a village clustered around a little bridge over a creek. A woman was doing her laundry in the creek, just downstream from the bridge. Alan slowed down, and turned into a small gap between two of the ramshackle huts that also served as retail stores.

A storekeeper rushed out, angry and about to admonish them, when he saw the 4x4 coming fast. He pulled a tarp across the gap, hiding the tuk-tuk, and then shooed away some curious children.

Just in time! Samphy and Harry zoomed past the hidden tuk-tuk and followed the road round the bend at the far end of the village.

Leng thanked the shopkeeper; Alan bowed and put some money in his hands. They took off, back across the same footpath and disappeared.

***

Harry aimed his gun at the tuk-tuk, waited for a smooth patch on the road, then fired.

"I thought you needed him alive," Samphy said.

"So did I. But Humboldt figured it out—before he went AWOL—that I really just need his thumb."

Samphy didn't get it. Harry ignored him and fired again, but by then the tuk-tuk had left the road and was somehow managing to stay on a footpath that ran between rice paddies and led to a little settlement at a bridge on a creek.

Samphy and Harry took the long way around but soon raced through the little village raising dust. They almost hit some people and provoked an angry gesture from a man in front of a little shop. They left the village, came round a bend and cursed: a long, straight, and very empty road lay ahead. Harry yelled at Samphy, and they raced back to the village only to find that the shopkeeper had blocked the bridge with his truck. He had the hood open and was working on the engine. Samphy and Harry arrived at the bridge, yelled at the shopkeeper, and then yelled louder and made threatening gestures when he acted dumb.

Samphy got out, grabbed a young child, and pointed his gun at the boy's head.

There was dead silence all around as if no one could believe that anyone could stoop this low. The boy started wailing; Samphy yelled at the shopkeeper. He closed the hood, got in, and moved his truck. The boy cried louder.

Bang! A shot rang out, and Samphy collapsed. A villager stepped out from the shadows and aimed his gun at Harry. Harry raised his arms.

Harry, hands still raised, shifted into the driver's seat of the 4x4, pressed the gas pedal, and steered over the bridge using his elbows. He took off without a second glance at Samphy.

***

Waiting in the formal reception area, Betty and Sakda looked out of place. Kareem entered smiling and said, "Welcome to the Royal Batari Embassy." Then he stopped and frowned. "Where's Alan?"

"We think he's on his way here." Betty said.

Kareem nodded and offered them refreshments. Betty was impatient, but Sakda, and Arab hospitality, helped keep her calm. Finally Alan called from the road. He and Leng had "borrowed" a truck—taking after Rithy?—and had raced most of the way to Phnom Penh. They'd soon be in the city, and Alan had a plan to get past the authorities.

Kareem was delighted with the news. He led Betty and Sakda to the tech room, a small office full of computers and telecom equipment. She took out the OPAL key fob and plugged it into a laptop. "I'm ready for Alan," she said and glanced outside. The embassy was surrounded by curious people. Betty worked at the laptop, paused and clicked Send. "Okay, a video compilation of Kapono's murder is out. I've tied it to PharmaGate."

She looked outside again and wondered how long it would take for her news release to show up out there. Then she looked past the regular people and noticed that soldiers had blocked all access points as police patrols moved into the streets beyond, creating an ever-expanding cordon around the embassy.

***

Keat Chhon gave orders to the police and soldiers in the square in front of the embassy. Civilians were held back but looked on from the nearby streets. Harry tried to get out of the crowd; Keat waved him back, and he melted into the shadows beside the embassy.

The civilians were suddenly focused on their phones, talking with each other in mutual shock. The soldiers and police broke ranks to find out what was on their screens. Keat should have dealt with the lack of discipline, but he too gave in to curiosity, whipped out his own phone, and saw that yet another breaking story was out. "Trade Envoy in Murder Video." He looked for but couldn't find Harry.

Keat looked less sure with each headline; he had to find a way out of this mess. The insurrection continued as more and more soldiers joined the people or pulled out their own phones. The mass of people grew and moved into the square, shouting and pointing at their screens. Keat watched them, and then made a decision.

***

Minutes before the security cordon had encompassed the derelict, half-built Gold Tower 42, Alan and Leng arrived at the flimsy gate and found Yuying. She'd paid off the single guard—with the equivalent of a month's wages at the local Nike factory—to go have lunch. The Gold Tower 42 was supposed to be Phnom Penh's highest building, but construction had stalled in 2008, and it had turned into a lingering monument to the financial crash of the same year. Other towers, like the Vattanac on the other side of central Phnom Penh, had risen above it in the meantime. They'd had better financing.

Alan went to kiss Yuying, but she pointed to the cage car of the construction elevator. Alan and Leng carried the paraglider into the elevator, and Yuying closed the door. She worked the controls, and they slowly went up. Alan let go a big breath of relief then inhaled her scent. "Thank you," he said.

"You're crazy," she replied, and they argued all the way up.

At the top, Yuying pulled the stop lever and held the door open for them to get out to the roof. The brisk wind was causing an updraft. Far below and a ways away, the Tonlé Sap and Mekong Rivers almost gift wrapped Phnom Penh.

Leng peered down at the army and police now flooding into the area and laughed. "They look down, not look up."

"This is beyond risky," Yuying said.

"And it's our best chance." Alan unpacked the paraglider then gauged the wind speed and direction and paced out the length of the roof. He toyed with his amulet and decided that he had to make a risky reverse takeoff. Going for him was the strong wind, his two helpers, and the height; it was better not to think about what was going against him. Leng helped him with the glider harness, and he turned on the sports cam attached to his helmet.

"Forget the documentary, just stay alive," Yuying said.

Alan grinned back then got serious. He faced toward the sail and directed Yuying and Leng to spread it out and hold the sides up. It billowed then went taut, pulling Alan forward.

He ran with the wind until his legs ran out of roof, then he abruptly dropped. Yuying and Leng raced to the edge and peered over, just in time to see Alan skillfully recover as he caught the updraft then managed to stabilize the sail. He regained altitude and sailed away.

Alan flew over the nearby Eclipse Bar, the original rooftop view-bar in Phnom Penh. The lone staff member cleaning the empty bar couldn't believe her eyes. Alan smiled at her and headed across the city. Despite the close call and the dire circumstances, Alan inhaled the complex urban smells and enjoyed the aerial views of Phnom Penh.

Clearing the Air

Betty worked furiously at the laptop. "The main research paper is ready to go. We just need Alan's thumbprint to release the core data and more video." Kareem smiled with her. Then she held her breath, did a final check, clicked and punched the air. "I sent the back story out," she said and looked outside.

"There's more," a barang lady shouted to the crowd in front of the embassy. Together they watched her screen scroll the headlines.

Betty watched the crowd while following the same feed on her own screen:

"Agarwood: Toxic or Miracle Cure?" - *Time*.

"Hundreds of Bataris Cured by Agarwood" - Médecins Sans Frontières.

"New Agarwood Info: Reprieve or Death Sentence for Old Growth Forests?" - *Nature*.

A buzz picked up among the people; more and more ignored their screens and looked up. Alan sailed across the sky. Shots rang out; not all of the army was distracted. Keat Chhon ordered the soldiers to stop, not to shoot. He was partly successful.

***

Just a few more shots were fired, but these bullets pierced Alan's sail. He pulled hard, trying to bank right to get to the embassy roof, but he couldn't make it. He turned hard left, glided away from the embassy, and descended to the side street below.

As Alan began to execute another graceful landing, Harry appeared from the shadows and grabbed at a trailing cord. Alan crashed hard, tangled in his gear; Harry jumped on him. He grabbed Alan's hand then pulled out a knife. He stopped, looked at Alan's

136

other hand, and yelled, "Which one?"

"Huh?" Alan was bruised and winded.

"Which thumb? For the OPAL."

Alan laughed through his pain. Sakda rushed out of the embassy's back door.

"Okay, I'll take both."

"You loser. We've got the key. It's over."

Sakda barreled into Harry and knocked him off Alan. Keat Chhon came round the corner, followed by a crowd of soldiers and civilians. He directed his men to seize Harry. Sakda freed Alan from the sail and helped him up. Alan took a deep breath, glad to get away from Harry's stench, and checked his sports cam.

Harry tried to ward off his captors by brandishing a piece of paper. "I have an international warrant for Grace."

Keat grabbed the paper, while his men cuffed Harry. Harry spit at Keat. "Turncoat! The eternal survivor switches sides again."

"Stay focused," Keat mocked back.

At Keat's gesture, his men dragged Harry away. Keat turned and smiled at Alan. "Dr. Grace, please." He ushered Alan toward the embassy back door and helped him as he limped up the steps. Betty was waiting there. "Thank you," Keat said. "Please remain a guest of King Kareem until we"—he rattled the arrest warrant—"straighten this out." He turned, gave orders to his men, and began to reestablish his authority.

"Thank heavens you're okay … but we're not finished." Betty was very focused.

"I know." Alan proffered his thumb.

She pulled him inside, steered him into the little office, and pointed at the laptop with the OPAL fob. Alan placed his thumb on the fob.

Nothing happened. They shared a look of alarm ... then Alan sheepishly shook his head. He put his other thumb on the OPAL.

CHIME.

Betty yelped in delight and made flourishing keystrokes. "Done! It's out! Agarwood for everyone, eh?"

Alan collapsed into a chair, let out a big breath, and grinned. Betty pointed at the crowd outside.

"Incoming." The barang lady in front of the embassy stared at her phone. Many people crowded around her, and more looked at their own phones.

Alan and Betty alternated between reading the headlines on the laptop and watching the crowd outside react to them.

"Smuggler releases data. Claims it obsoletes smuggling and clear-cutting" - *CNN*

"Plantations can produce medical grade agarwood per exonerated fugitive" - *Bloomberg*

A huge buzz erupted across the square and beyond.

Alan started to celebrate with Betty and Sakda. Leng and Yuying arrived and joined in. Hard to believe it was over, they all agreed. Yuying hugged Alan close. Kareem came in, and she stepped back.

Alan sobered up. "Tell Nazneen—"

"It's okay. She'll be fine." Kareem looked around, nodding and smiling gratefully at all of them, including Yuying.

Alan rubbed his amulet and struggled to understand his own emotions. "I'm a scientist."

"She understands."

"If I were a prince..."

Kareem smiled and winked at him. "You're a hunter!"

Epilogue: Snapshots

I first learned about Alan's adventures from the worldwide frenzy that dominated both mainstream and social media for a few days. Now, of course, the spotlight has moved on. All the salacious details have been used up, the bigger issues ignored.

I rushed to Cambodia to see Alan, recorded his amazing tale, then collected stories from Leng, Sakda, Betty, Yuying, Kareem, and Nazneen. It was quite the trek to find Chief Rithy, but eventually I got his side of the story, too. We watched the trials of Wilkes and Bondwell broadcast from the US. Humboldt was still AWOL, and Harry had vanished. They'd sent a plane to extract him from Cambodia before he could be charged. It simply disappeared … after they'd picked him up.

***

The months after Alan left the embassy were busy and productive. Alan and Betty evangelized the new growing and distilling methods for domesticated agarwood, and we all helped invest the agarwood fortune in Maran.

Leng and Alan helped finish the new schoolhouse. Around us the houses all had new metal roofs, and other villagers did roadwork as the village got paved. I filmed it all with my cam.

I glanced down the road; two nurses arrived at the new clinic that had sprung up next to the repaired bridge over the river. Betty and Sakda greeted them then headed into the trees for another jungle-skills lesson.

Later we all gathered in the little graveyard to put flowers on three new graves; Kapono's was in the middle.

***

Nazneen looked splendid in a fashionable business suit. "Congratulations," I said. She passed through the lobby and entered the boardroom to accept her appointment as the new CEO of Arabian Scents.

I smiled at Alan and Kareem. Kareem pointed toward the front door where a second corporate identity was being installed on the masthead: Princess Potions Rx.

***

Alan and I nursed cold Angkor beers and watched the sun set from the balcony of the famous FCC. Unlike its namesake clubs in other Asian power centers, the Phnom Penh Foreign Correspondents Club is simply a popular restaurant-bar at the confluence of the Tonlé Sap and Mekong Rivers. He pointed at a passing tuk-tuk below on the street and laughed. "That's the export inspector … with his gorgeous companion!"

My phone pinged with an incoming message. It was a short video clip from Betty. She was sitting next to Rithy in his hut. They wore identical headphones and nodded together in rhythm, sharing her music.

Yunnan

Fan drove Yuying and Alan up a hill to a gate on a remote road. It had a sign in Chinese along with the English translation: Yunnan Agarwood Agricultural Collective. They got out.

Yuying said, "See, we really exist … and we need your help."

"And here I thought you just wanted my body."

"Well," she said, grinning, "I waited long enough."

Yuying anointed Alan with oil; Alan inhaled and looked

impish. While Yuying stared at him, incredulous, he chanted, childlike:

"The Christian calls it eagle wood,

To the Muslim it is oud.

Whatever name for agarwood,

It always lifts my … mood."

They laughed together. "It was worth waiting for," Yuying said and moved in to take advantage of Alan's "lifted mood."

***

I approached the hillside in a helicopter—rented by the Documentary Channel—and saw Yuying with Alan. I immediately started filming; the rest of the film crew would soon arrive by road to finish the new documentary. On my cam screen, I saw the two lovers embrace and kiss. Wow. I imagined a feature-film ending to this story…

From a bird's eye view, the road wound through the hilly jungle, past the lovers to a primitive plantation in various shades of green, patches of seedlings next to plots of mature trees. A few workers tended the trees.

From higher and higher up, Alan and Yuying faded to a tiny speck, then were gone. From space it was just the beautiful blue planet.

Fade to black while music played.

***

But back on Earth, the music got louder and Yuying got annoyed. "Alan? Who is that?" She pointed at the approaching vehicle blasting music. "And that?" Even more annoyed, she pointed up at the loud helicopter.

"Oh, yeah." Alan went for his amulet and inhaled. "I forgot to mention…"

The helicopter swooped past, and the film crew arrived blaring the latest music from Dengue Fever.

.

Images

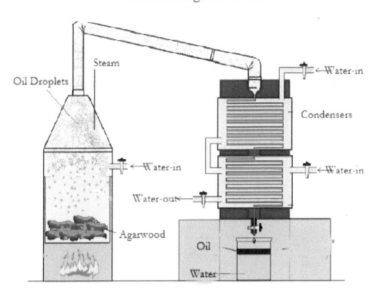

Agarwood Distiller: By Hafizmuar from English Wikipedia

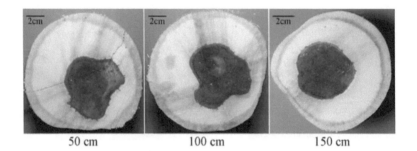

50 cm   100 cm   150 cm

Domestic Agarwood Samples

http://www.mdpi.com/1420-3049/18/3/3086

Wild Agarwood Chip and Beads

Alan Mahaffey

Acronyms, etc.

CIA: Central Intelligence Agency (USA)

FDA: Food and Drug Administration (USA)

DIA: Defense Information Agency (USA)

NSA: National Security Agency (USA)

DEA: Drug Enforcement Agency (USA)

UNTAC: United Nations Transitional Authority in Cambodia (1992-93)

OPAL FOB: A (fictional) widget that plugs into a computer USB port. It provides fingerprint security access to protected files on the computer and in the cloud.

Acknowledgments

First in line for acknowledgement is Alan Mahaffey—the real-life inspiration for the very fictional Alan Grace. Alan introduced me to Agarwood. See *Facts and Fictions* below for more about Alan.

Many thanks to my early readers for their patience and valuable feedback:

Tihemme Gagnon—who read the first version when it was a fledgling screenplay and gave me great plot and character suggestions. (Vancouver Community College)

Mark Timko and Trudy Austin also read and helped out with the screenplay version.

Juan Cole for answering an Arabian Gulf related question. (www.juancole.com)

Trudy, Danielle and Paul Austin and Boris Sin who all struggled through the first draft of the novella and pointed the right way to go.

Chris Beck, Kevin Keeler and especially Ann Cowan who gave great feedback on a later draft. Ann convinced me to find a copy editor.

David Antrobus, my fantastic copy editor who corrected my mistakes and made great suggestions. I was lucky to find David via a listing of copy editors. You can find him at https://bewritethere.com/.

Facts and Fiction

Most of the information about the agarwood in the book is true. Cultivated agarwood from plantations is a key ingredient in much of the incense we burn and many of the Asian, Arabic, or western fragrances we use. The wild *Aquilaria* trees that agarwood comes from are either already lost to clear-cutting poachers or under threat across Southeast Asia. What's left of these trees are now under CITES protection, for what it's worth. Wild agarwood is among the most expensive substances on earth. Poaching and smuggling are common.

There is a real wild-agarwood trader named Alan Mahaffey. I did meet him on a bus ride from Bangkok to Trat, Thailand on the way to Koh Chang. At the time, he was considering a job offer to manage an agarwood plantation. (He did not accept the offer.) He will not buy from the clear-cutters; his agarwood comes from the forest floor and he's a much nicer guy than Alan Grace. You can learn more about him (and watch a documentary!) at this link: https://www.agarwoodconsulting.com/

Agarwood oil and leaves have long been used as medicine. There is new interest in using the leaves to treat illness. The possibility of the "miracle cure" aspect is a little like some of the debate surrounding medical cannabis, either fictional or speculative, depending on your point of view.

Batar is a fictional Arab Gulf State. Perhaps you can imagine it nestled in among Qatar, Bahrain, Dubai, UAE, Kuwait, Iran, and Saudi Arabia?

The Maran village and valley, and the Teuk Vet Waterfalls are fictional but set in the very real Cardamom Mountains in southwestern Cambodia.

The remnants of the Khmer Loeu hill tribes do exist and live in the northern highlands of Cambodia; their presence in the Cardamom region may be fictional.

Fat Sam's in Koh Kong is real. They have great food and good gossip.

The kind of party-hut situation described in the book can be found around Asia. There are many beach-party places in Thailand and Cambodia. The backpacker party scene that directly inspired Xanadu in this novel actually flourished on the Nam Song River in Vang Vieng, Laos, for a number of years. After the deaths of many young backpackers, the Laos government reacted to international pressure and tamed the party.

A request from the author:

Independent books need Reader Reviews!

Please post a few comments about my book at Amazon.com or Goodreads.com.

Thanks .. Ron

Made in United States
Troutdale, OR
10/08/2024

23569508R00094